Second Chances

New Hope Series, Volume 1

Wendy Varnadore

Published by Wendy Varnadore, 2021.

SECOND CHANCES

First edition. May 4, 2021.

ISBN: 979-8201676865

Written by Wendy Varnadore.

To my Mom,my biggest supporter. Wish you were
here now.

Love,

Wendy

Prologue

They had met their first night on board and spend most of the trip in each other's company. Nicole was on the cruise for her best friend's elopement, and other than the time that claimed she was free.

She'd been standing on the deck, alone, looking at the stars. He'd approached her and told her a romantic story of the couple of constellations that circled the North Star. Jason was handsome, charming, and intelligent. She had been flattered by his attentions from the beginning. It had been a long time since she felt she held a man's undivided attention.

On board they had swam together, shared drinks in the hot tub, danced together, and walked miles around the deck, just talking. While on the island they had picnicked on the beach and explore the stores.

The night before had been the last night on board and she had been tired of fighting what was between them. After dancing for a couple of hours, her heart racing and skin on fire where he touched, she had invited him back to her room for drinks on her balcony. Before they had finished a glass of wine a piece they had been in each other's arms.

She had let his kisses drag her into a night of passion like she'd never known. They had driven each other wild with kisses and caresses while making love three times. She would never forget their time together, or regret taking her mother's advice, but she couldn't break a promise already made to another.

She slid from his embrace as easily as she could, and dressed quicky in the shorts and top she'd left out for that purpose. Then she looked down at him, once last time. They had shared no last names, no hometowns, there would be no finding him if she walked away now.

She didn't know what she was afraid of the most if he woke before she left; that he would convince her to break her promise or that he wouldn't even try. Her heart turned over slowly at the thought of never seeing him again and it had only been a week. If she took a chance and he tired of her before she did him, it would hurt her more than she could bare.

She convinced herself that it was better this way. Broken promises caused people to be hurt. That's the one lesson she learned from her father and she wouldn't be like him.

She would treasure their time together, the things he'd made her feel, but if he was a temptation she couldn't afford. She would leave the dream here and return to the real world, where she had already chosen her path.

With a sigh of regret she left, closing the door softly behind her.

WHEN JASON WOKE, HE would have thought he had a very life-like dream, but he wasn't in his own cabin. As he dressed and looked around the empty cabin he cursed. He had never meant for her to get away, no matter the deal they had.

Running to his own cabin to grab his luggage, thankfully he'd packed the day before, he noticed everyone getting ready to disembark. After grabbing his bag, he dashed all over the ship, but had no luck.

He'd never met anyone that interested him as much as she did. He usually tired of a lady after a couple of dates, but they had spent countless hours together and he still wanted to see more of her. Even making love with her had been beyond his wildest expectations.

When it was time for him to leave the ship, he did so with a heavy heart and a vow- he would find her somehow. The strawberry blond that stole his heart the first time he'd seen her

Chapter One

With a heavy sigh Nicole pushed her chair away from her desk. Getting up she walked over to stare out the window in her office. It was no use. You just couldn't find someone with just their first name.

Hadn't she known ten years ago how difficult it would be if she tried? She had no regrets about her decision, she'd done the only thing she could and look herself in the mirror.

She had locked herself in her office, telling no one to disturb her four days ago. She knew that her employees, and her business partner and friend, were curious to know what she was doing. She usually had an open-door policy at the bookstore/cafe.

She had been a widow for eight years now and people were, not so subtly, letting her know it was time to get back out there. In the past she'd been satisfied with her business and raising her son, but even she had to admit that it got lonely.

She'd been dreaming of someone from her past and decided to look them up but it wasn't going well. They met on the cruise she had taken when helping her best friend, Summer. elope. After the ceremony she'd left the newlyweds to themselves and walked the deck. The night had been clear and she'd stopped by the railing to look at the stars over the water. He'd approached and started pointing out constellations, and telling her Greek myths about them.

After that night they had spent the rest of the cruise in the others company, when she wasn't obligated elsewhere, and enjoyed themselves a great deal. They had danced and enjoyed the ship at night and took day trips on the islands. But she'd left knowing only first names and exchanging no phone numbers or addresses. This wasn't the first time she'd wondered if it had been a mistake to leave it that way.

A knock on her office door brought her back to the present. She called for them to enter as she went over and re-took her seat. She was surprised when her best friend and business partner popped around the door and put a cup of coffee in front of her.

"Summer, you never knock."

The blond took a chair across from the desk. "You seem unusually busy this week. Is there

anything I can help with?"

She and Summer were lifelong friends, no one knew her better, so Nicole knew what she was really asking. "Not unless you can find someone with only a first name and vague idea of their life, no hard details."

"You would have asked by now if you thought I did." Summer sat back in her chair. "Who are you trying to find?"

"No one that you know."

"Would it be that dark, handsome someone you spent time with on my elopement?" Summer inquired with a knowing smile.

Nicole's eyes widened. "You knew? And you never said anything?"

Summer laughed. "It may have seemed as if we were in a world built for two, but I knew what was going in with you. We even saw you two together a couple of times."

"You never approached."

"You didn't wear your engagement ring," Summer turned serious. "I didn't know what was going on but if you were leaving your options open, I wasn't going to stand in the way of that."

"I'm not sure what I was doing, either, except doing as my mother ask." Nicole admitted. "She made me promise that I would go on that trip as if I were single, to not settle for what I had grown comfortable with."

"Well, tell me what he was like. Must be pretty special for\ you to be thinking of him ten year later." Summer commented. "Especially if you're trying to find him."

"Honestly, I left the ring home to humor Mom. She thought the whole cruise would be like an old episode of 'The Love Boat'. I never thought I would actually meet someone." Nicole began, thinking back. "His name was Jason and he was thoughtful, intelligent, and kind. We discussed everything under the sun, even debated a few times, with him usually winning me over."

Smiling slightly, she continued, "He made me feel carefree, like I could be myself. He also made my pulse race when he took my hand, or put his arm around me. I couldn't believe he wanted to spend all his time with me. And the first time we kissed was unlike anything I've ever known; I grew breathless and weak, like they describe in novels."

"Were the two of you intimate?" Summer broke in.

Nicole felt herself blush a she answered, "Only once. The last night. Then I left while he slept and came back to my life."

Summer's mouth opened, she quickly shut it, then opened again. "Why?"

Nicole fidgeted with a pen laying on her desk. "I had broken a promise, Summer, and you know how I feel about that. Taking the engagement ring off didn't change that."

"So, you felt guilty."

"And David was the safer choice. I knew that I could never hurt him." Nicole admitted, "If Jason was feeling even a tenth of what I was I didn't want to hurt him by explaining there could never be a future for us."

They spent the next few minutes in silence; Summer thinking everything over and Nicole waiting for her reaction.

"Maybe it wasn't Jason that you were afraid would get hurt." Summer suggested. "Maybe you were afraid you would get hurt."

"Why would you say that?"

"Why else would you skip out on a man that you describe as kind for a man that disrespected you at every turn."

"I told you that just because the symbol of my promise wasn't with me didn't mean that I forgot that I had made one."

Shrugging Susan asked, "So what's got you looking for him?"

Narrowing her eyes Nicole replied, "When your mother-in-law teams up with your mother to set you up it doesn't take much to make you realize how pathetic you must seem."

"No one thinks that you're pathetic." Summer told her, then grinned, "When did you figure it out?"

"Not long after they started interviewing for T.J.'s tutor." Thoams was her son, named after his grandfather, and so bright that he was years ahead of other children his age. His Grandmother's had decided to find him a tutor in his favorite subject for the summer. "You should see the resumes of the ones they have rejected."

"That doesn't explain why you have decided to hunt up a man you haven't thought of in ten years." Noting the blush Nicole felt heating her cheeks, her friend added, "Unless you have thought about him."

"Not often. It felt wrong while David was still alive. Then I was busy with T.J. and starting the business." she admitted. "Since I figured out what was really going on, I admitted to myself that I'm lonely. But, as you know, no one around here interest me."

"And you thought of Jason."

Nicole nodded, "And I haven't been able to stop, so I decided to try finding him, but I've found nothing. Of course, he could be married by now anyway."

"If you found him and he was still single, what had you planned to do?"

"I thought about contacting him, to see if he wanted to meet. To see if things were the way I remember them." *See if he can still make me shiver with the slightest touch, if he can make me feel warm with just a glance*, she thought to herself.

"Well, I'm sorry you couldn't find him."

"Did I tell you they finally chose a tutor?" Nicole changed the subject. "He's an Environmental psychist that's recently agreed to a job at Georgia Tech."

"When is he arriving?"

"By lunch tomorrow." Nicole answered, looking through some orders on her desk. "I promised to be there when he arrives so I'll be taking an early day."

"We can handle it. Just be sure to call me and let me know how it goes."

JASON STOOD BY THE bed in the room he grew up in, trying to remember what he was forgetting to pack. Since he'd spent more time traveling than in Atlanta, he'd decided he didn't need his own place, and stayed with his father when in town. He decided it was time to settle around his

family since his father was getting older, and started as a professor at Georgia Tech in August.

Since he couldn't stay idyll that long, he'd decided to tutor a young genius in the small, neighboring town of New Hope. His father and brothers were encouraging him to take some time off but he couldn't do that, his mind wouldn't let him. Much like the boy he'd agreed to tutor and mentor, his mind needed a puzzle to solve.

He wasn't surprised when the knock on his door was followed by his younger brother sticking his head in.

"Come on in." He told Seth.

Seth walked in and leaned against the dresser. "Looks as if you're all ready," he commented.

Looking around the room one more time he admitted. "I feel as if I'm forgetting something."

Seth looked around and came up with a small photo album laying on the dresser. "What about this?"

It was only a four by six album with a few family pictures but mostly with pictures of his graduation trip. He'd taken it with him everywhere since then. Seth tossed it to him, and he neatly caught it. As he stared at the picture showing through the cover he wondered again where she was. He put the album in his night stand drawer.

Seth's eyes grew wide. "You're not taking it?"

"I carry family pictures in my wallet." Jason replied, dryly.

"But what about the one that got away?"

That was how his brothers referred to the woman he'd met on that trip. He could still picture her with the moonlight shining off her strawberry blond hair, and the interested look in her eye as he explained his studies. "Maybe it's time to give up on lost dreams."

Seth's mouth dropped open. It had been ten years since that trip and in all of his travels for work he'd carried that album and looked for her in every city, disappointed every time. But he

was moving home, with little chance of ever finding her, and he had to accept that it wasn't meant to be.

Having found his voice Seth remarked, "I never thought you would give up on finding her."

Jason sat on his small bed. "There was little chance of ever finding her, now the chance is smaller."

"You know we never understood why you hung on to the dream of her when you had beautiful woman vying for your attention."

Jason knew that the ladies admired his body. He worked out regularly and ate healthy. He was trim and well-muscled, with black hair and grey eyes. "Yes, they like the looks of me, and I obviously please them in bed, but when I try to talk about my work, I can see their eyes glaze over."

"And this Nicole wasn't like that."

Shaking his head, he smiled at the memory. "She would get this light of interest on her eyes and would ask questions when she didn't understand something. She was smart and loved to talk about literature, explaining things about it that I never understood until then."

"Did you fall in love with her?"

"I don't know." Jason lied, then tossing in a bit of truth, "I'm not sure what it would feel like. I'm familiar with the different types of love and felt them all, except eros love. I do know she made me feel things I'd never felt before or since."

"What were you going to do if you found her?"

"If she was available, I was going to explore things further, find out why she walked out on me."

"Are you giving up on her or love altogether?"

"Maybe I'm not capable of that emotion." Jason admitted his greatest fear. "If it weren't for my three brothers dragging me out to make sure that I had all experiences I would be more emotionally stunted than I am."

"What are you talking about?"

Heaving a sigh, he began to try to explain. "I feel the basic emotions- happiness, hate, fear, anger, and sadness, but it's dimmed when compared to what I've seen in others."

"Are you saying that she was your only shot for real love?" Seth questioned, "Because I don't believe that's true. I think you've had your mind on finding her that you never truly considered anyone after that."

Jason stood and closed his suitcase. "She just seemed to understand me, or want to try at least. I guess that I'll never find out." But even as he said it, he didn't truly believe that.

He didn't believe in fate but he did believe there were people, like himself, that found it hard to connect with many people on an emotional level. He'd found that connection once. He just wasn't sure that he would find another.

Seth slapped him on the shoulder. "Who knows? Maybe this single mother of a genius will grab your attention."

Jason was to remember those words a couple of hours later.

Pulling in to the driveway of his home for the next few months, Jason was stuck, once again, with a since of wonder. The house was as close to a mansion as he'd ever seen in a small town. Red brick with two wings branching off of the foyer and staircase.

When he rang the bell, he wasn't greeted by a maid as he expected, but as the two ladies that interviewed him. Rose was a tall slender woman with silver streaking her raven hair. Jean was shorter, with brown hair and a smile that reminded him of someone that he couldn't place. They were T.J.'s grandmothers, and very welcoming as they showed him to a small den.

"We're glad to see you made good time." Rose said, as she sat on a delicate sofa. "I know traffic from the city on the weekends can be terrible."

"T.J. is very excited." Jean put in. "I do hope you're prepared for him. He never seems to slow down."

Jason chuckled. "I was the same way, driving my parents crazy."

The maid arrived with iced tea for all of them and exited quickly, as Rose thanked her.

"So, you know what to expect." Jean smiled again, making him wish he could figure out who it reminded him of. It was tickling the back of his mind persistently. "My daughter should be arriving shortly. She went into the store for a couple of hours but promised she would return before lunch."

"I'm sure that meeting her will be as much a pleasure as it was meeting the two of you." he replied, smoothly.

Just then the dark haired nine-year-old ran into the room, and straight to his side. "You're finally here."

"I'm glad that you're ready because I have a lot of plans for this summer." Jason told him.

T.J. turned to his grandmothers. "Can I show him where we'll be working while we're waiting on Mom?"

"He may want to rest after his trip..." Rose began, but Jason stopped her by standing up.

"I need to move around after that drive, if you don't mind."

"Of course, then, T.J. do him the honors." Rose permitted.

He followed the young boy out of the room and down the wing to the right. T.J. led him into the first door on the right, which turned out to be a study. There was a long picture window with the dark curtain pulled back to let the sun shine on a large wood desk of mahogany.

The wall to the right was covered with bookcases, with ever shelve full. As the young boy pointed out their section, he took note of how well stocked they already were, as well as organized.

"What's your favorite area of physics?" Jason asked him.

"For now, it's astronomy." T.J. answered.

"That's my favorite as well." Jason confided. "But I went onto Environmental Physicists because I could be more help to people."

As they headed back to the den, they continued talking about the subjects they would try to cover in the time they had, as well as the problems with the environment. Just outside of the door he heard a tinkle of female laughter that stopped him in his tracks. When his hearted started beating again he smiled at his own foolishness. It couldn't possibly be who he thought it was.

He entered as the newest female turned to greet her son, and lost his breath. Her strawberry blond hair was cut in a shorter style and she'd gained some fuller curves, he assumed from giving birth, but it was her. He could never forget those blue green eyes and her rounded chin that made her face appear heart shaped.

He didn't hear the boy introduce him, but when she looked up to greet him, she froze as well.

But only for moment, as she smiled and shook his hand. Her hand was warm in his and he felt

the tremor that she couldn't hide from him.

He managed a low, "Pleasure to meet you."

"I've heard a lot about you Mr. Matthews, or is it Professor?" she withdrew her hand as she spoke.

"Jason will do. No need to be formal. "

"I'm Nicole. We aren't formal around here either, as I'm sure that you've learned by now." she replied. "I'm just going to wash up before I join you at the table."

It amused him that she was getting away to collect her thoughts. He almost wished he could do the same as he followed everyone else into the dining room. Pictures of long past ancestors hung on the wall, along with pictures of the house in different stages of its life. A large dining table and China cabinet of oak looked to be antiques, but the chairs appeared more modern.

As they took their seats Rose sat at the head of the table with Jean and T.J. on one side. The other seat to Rose's side was left for Nicole, as that was her usual seat, and Jason at her side. He sensed something going on behind the seating arrangement, but his thoughts of having found her, just when he'd given up looking, wouldn't allow for anything else.

When she swept back into the room she didn't even pause before taking her seat. As the rest made small talk Jason absorbed the feeling of just being near her again. She was cheerful, covering her nervousness with chatter, and still smelled of strawberries. The years didn't matter, nothing did, all he wanted was to see if she still she tasted as sweet as her scent implied.

Then she turned to him, "I've been told you were traveling for work. What made you choose to settle in Atlanta?"

"It's where I'm from. My brothers and Dad are still there."

"And your mother."

"She left when we were still young." he replied, softly. That wasn't a subject he talked about, or even thought about.

"Were you hoping to find her in your travels." she asked, her voice soft.

He trapped her blue green eyes with his, "No, not her."

He noticed her intake of breath before he turned his attention to what her son was telling him. As he listened to the young boy, he began to do some math in his head, and as he did, he began drawing some conclusions that he didn't like.

He was about to ask her when they could talk privately when the maid arrived with the phone.

"I'm sorry to disturb your meal but it's Ms. Summer and says it's urgent that she speak to Ms. Nicole."

Rose nodded and the young lady gave Nicole the cordless phone and hurried back into the kitchen.

"What is it, Summer?"

He knew that Summer was not only Nicole's business partner, but also her life-long friend and he wondered if she had planned this interruption.

"I'm sorry." Nicole said to them. "There's a problem with an order and I need to get back." She turned to Jason. "Welcome and I'll see you this evening."

He barely had time to stand before he was watching her make her escape, or so she thought.

Chapter Two

Nicole walked into the front door of the store and straight to her office, leaving the door open for Summer. She had promised her an explanation, after all. Wringing her hands together, she took a calming breath and heard the door shut softly behind her.

Turning, she found Summer leaned against the door with her arms folded over her chest. "You said you were taking the afternoon off to acquaint yourself with T.J.'s tutor."

"Oh, we're already acquainted." she replied, wringing her hands.

"What does that mean?" Summer stepped forward to take her hands into her own.

"You know how people say when you stop looking for something it'll turn up." She waited for Summer to nod before finishing. "Guess who turned up?"

She watched Summer's blue eyes grow wide and when she spoke her voice was disbelieving, "You're joking."

"No. It turns out that Jason Matthews hails from Atlanta and has come home to settle down near his family after traveling for work in disaster areas for F.E.M.A."

Summer walked over to the chair in front of the desk. "That close. What did you do?"

Taking her own chair, she covered her face with her hands. "I introduced myself as if we'd never met."

"I take it that you didn't fool him."

"Never thought I would but he played along. But as we ate and talked, I could see that he was thinking some things over and they weren't making him happy."

"I've never known you to run away."

"No, but if there's going to be a confrontation, I don't want everyone there to hear it. If I'm lucky I can get him to agree to stay for my son's sake." She could still see him at lunch, watching the older man, and trying to mimic his gestures. "I can't take this away from him. He's been so excited."

"So, you expect him to follow you here?" Summer was stunned. "What about the employees?"

"When he comes in, I need you to turn the music up, maybe that will help. And if not, I'll be the talk of the town tomorrow."

"Hate to break it to you but people have talked about you for a while now."

"Because of things David done, not because of me."

"What are you going to tell him?"

Nicole sighed. "The truth. I'm just not sure how he's going to take it?"

"Most men would be honored to be an attractive woman's last fling before getting married." Summer commented.

"From the look on his face Jason isn't going to be one of them." Nicole replied, dryly. "I can't believe I never thought of this when I was looking for him."

"Because you would have had time to explain, and now he's just going to demand it. Angrily, if you're right." Just then Jason opened the office door and glared at Nicole. Summer stood and whispered, "Good luck."

Jason stepped inside to allow Summer to leave before shutting it, forcefully. "So, you did orchestrate this."

Nicole stood. "Yes, I was hoping you would follow."

"You don't want your family to know about us." he remarked, harshly. "Are you ashamed that you were slumming it while on vacation?"

Choosing to ignore the snide comment, she said, "I just thought it would be more private here. Why don't you have a seat and we can talk about this?"

He walked over to the chair Summer had vacated and waited for her to sit first. She leaned on her desk and tried to stay serene in the face of his obvious fury. "I need you to promise that whatever is said here you consider not leaving this position. It would break my son's heart."

"I promise to consider it." he offered after a pause. "I thought if I saw you again my first question would be why you walked out the way you did, but I guess that I already know."

"What do you think that reason is?" She inquired, figuring this was a good place to start.

"How serious was your relationship when you decided to deceive him?"

"It's more complicated than that."

He shrugged, casually. "I'm not going anywhere."

"David and I started dating his Senior year of high school, I was a Junior He was the only serious relationship I'd ever been in. He proposed a few weeks before Summer's elopement."

"So, you were engaged?"

"Yes, and my mother worried that I was making a mistake. She requested for the duration of the trip I act as if I weren't in a relationship, to enjoy adult life as a single woman rather than settle down with the first man I dated. I agreed but I never expected to meet anyone, let alone someone that I found as interesting as I did you."

"So, you were using me and I never stood a chance." he stood and started pacing. "Of course not. Why would someone like you reach so far beneath her."

She stood and walked around her desk. "It wasn't like that. I was attracted to you and I loved our time together."

"Just not enough." His voice was getting louder and she was glad she had planned for it. "Just for future reference next time you decide to use a man's body, don't make him care about you."

"Jason," she began softly and reached out to touch his arm and tell him that she'd been hunting for him, but he jerked away.

He jerkily shook his head. "I've heard enough." Then he left her alone, slamming the door as he went.

JASON WENT FOR A DRIVE an ended up on a cliff that overlooked the small town. *Probably where the teenagers come to make out,* he thought bitterly. He'd never felt this weary before-like he couldn't breathe deeply enough and an odd emptiness in his chest. As if his lungs and heart were being pulled from him.

He'd never been good at reading people, but he'd never been this wrong about someone. He had thought she was a lovely woman looking for the right man. He never could have guessed that she'd just been out to have a fling.

Over the years when he thought about having a family like his older brothers, she was the one he'd pictured. Wondering if she'd ever thought of him the same way. It turns out she walked away and never gave him second thought.

His eyes stung and he realized it was from unshed tears. He couldn't remember the last time he'd cried. Probably when they'd come home from school to find an empty house and a letter from their mom saying that she was leaving. His chest felt hollow, as if something were missing there.

Getting out of the car he walked around it several times, trying to decide what to do, he couldn't think past this pain, that he couldn't name. Taking out his cell he dialed Seth's number. Seth was the youngest of the four of them, but no one understood him better.

"Hey, Bro. How's it going?" After not getting a response, his voice grew tense. "Jason, is something wrong?"

Finding his voice, Jason said, shortly, "She's here."

"Who's there?"

"Nicole is the boy's mother."

"You're joking." was the response. "I thought that would make you happy. Yet you sound disappointed."

Absently rubbing his chest, Jason remarked, and told him what he'd learned. "I think this feeling is far more than disappointment. Considering T.J.'s age I figured that she had been seeing someone then, and that's why she took off the way she did. She was using me."

"You don't know that." his brother cautioned. "That could be it but did you consider that she told you the truth and was exploring her options? If she had just wanted an affair, she would have had you on the first night. There was no reason for her to spend so much time getting to know you"

"That doesn't explain this feeling." he murmured, still rubbing his chest.

"What feeling?" Seth asked, sounding concerned again.

"I'm so angry that tears are burning my eyes and my chest feels hollow, and I can't take a deep breath." Jason knew he wouldn't tell anyone else that, but Seth was the one he always counted on.

"Well, big brother, the good news is that you're not as lacking in feelings of love as you thought." Seth told him. "The bad news is that feeling is heartbreak, and those tears are of loss, not anger."

"How do I stop it?" Even as he spoke, he knew there was nothing he could do.

Sure enough, Seth chuckled. "If I knew the answer to that I would be a rich man. Now why are you convinced that she was using you?"

"You remember me telling you about this house, and the servants, it's obvious she chose someone she never would in her real life."

"Then my question remains, why not the first night. You spent days together and were only intimate once. Maybe there are things you don't know yet, you should find out what they are."

"I really thought you would encourage me to come home." Jason was honesty surprised. "You've tried to talk me out of this from the beginning."

"I never stand in the way of someone in love." There was a silence, before he told him. "Don't give up on her. Don't leave yourself to wonder what if."

"I wasn't coming home anyway." Jason confessed. "I made a commitment and I'm going to stand by it. So, I'll think about what you said."

"Good luck. Wait until I tell our older brothers tonight." Seth laughed. "They'll never believe she was that close all of this time. I'll leave it to you to fill in the details of course."

"Thanks. I'll call in a couple of days."

He stood, leaning against the hood of his Taurus and thought over the events of the day. He knew talking to his brother would help him get over the hurdle and able to think things through.

Most of him said that if this was love and heart break, he didn't want any part of it. But that small part of him that yearned for a family of his own, told him that Seth was right, there was more to this story than what she was telling him.

But how to find out? And if she didn't care for him, would it be worth the pain?

FIVE DAYS LATER NICOLE was so wound tight that she didn't want to go home. Trying to eat had been a strain, as she still sat beside Jason. The two of them seldom spoke directly to the other. That didn't stop the goose bumps she got every time they accidently brushed hands. Her hands grew sweaty, causing her to drop things.

She was aware of the electricity between them, but wondered if he was. Being close to him, smelling his spicy scent of cloves, was giving her urges that she hadn't felt in years. She remembered the way it felt to be held by him, the taste of his kisses, and the feel of him under her hands. She wanted nothing more than to feel those things again.

But Jason gave no indication that he was feeling the same way. He spoke easily with the rest of the family, and seemed to have a good appetite. If he had moved past his hurt and anger, he hadn't told her, but she would suffer in silence before asking.

She knew why she felt that way. She felt guilty. The one thing she'd sworn never to do was hurt someone in that way. Not after watching what her mother went through when her father had finally taken off. She had seen it in his eyes and instantly wanted to make things right, but it was too late for that.

One thing she knew was that you couldn't turn back time and it was a waste of time thinking about how things could've been different. All she could do was apologize and give him his space, which wasn't easy when you had two people so determined to push them together.

There was a light knock on her office door before Summer walked in. "Everyone is gone for the day."

"Alright." She rose from her chair and was reaching for her purse when she got an idea. "Summer, why don't we have Girl's night tonight. Get some dinner, have a few drinks."

Summer raised a blond brow. "Is it that bad?"

"The guilt is." Nicole admitted. "The regret."

They walked through the store together. "You didn't hurt him intentionally." Summer tried to assure her.

"But the chance was there for someone to be hurt, and I ignored it."

"You didn't see it. There's a difference." Summer replied. "Let me call home and we'll go get some pizza."

Before long they were being served a medium pizza and cocktails. And Nicole unloaded it all on the only person she trusted.

"He's good with T.J. and both the mothers. I don't think they've noticed the tensions between us yet. I still dream about him. And not just the memories, but fantasies of the two of us now. He's still handsome and I find myself just watching him some times."

"Maybe you should try telling him that you had been searching for him." Summer suggested. "He may be willing to forget the past."

Nicole finished her third drink and shook her head. "I disgust him."

"I doubt that." Summer tried to caution her. "Maybe you should slow down on the drinks."

"I can't sleep. Did you know they put him practically across the hall from me?"

Summer giggled. "And he has no clue what they're up to?"

"Not as far as I can tell. But I remember that from before, when spoke of books he often didn't understand the plotting. I've noticed it in T.J., that's why I've insisted on a literary day in his studies. It's the best way I know to teach him certain lessons about human behavior."

They were soon joined by a few other ladies and Nicole decided to take a night from her worries and have fun. She was amazed to find that she was able to do just that, despite the odd looks she was getting from her old friends. She hadn't realized that she'd been so serious minded since becoming a widow.

It was close to midnight when Summer finally convinced her to leave. Nicole let her window down and let the wind blow on her face. "That was so much fun. Why don't we do it more often? Why did you let me become a stick in the mud?"

"Because you were grieving and I assumed you would come out of it. It just took longer than I thought." Summer answered, taking no offense. "The question is will it last?"

Closing her eyes and sighing, Nicole thought about it. "I don't know. I didn't know about that rumor about me."

"About a mysterious affair? People are going to talk and no one would have blame if you hooked up at David's funeral."

Nicole giggled as she pictured it. "I believe Mom would have cheered me on."

"People can't understand why you're trying to be so respectful of him, it's easier for them to believe a secret affair."

"I don't do it for him." she admitted. "I would never do anything to disrespect Rose or Thomas' memory."

"Apparently Rose would approve," was Summer's reply.

After a moment of silence. "I have to admit they did choose perfectly. Too bad it's not going to work out the way they hoped."

Pulling up in front of the large home Summer didn't answer, just got out to help her in since she was stumbling a bit. It was quiet, indicating that everyone was in their rooms for the night.

They managed to make it to her room before she stumbled into a table in the hallway and knocked the vase of flowers off, causing it to shatter. The door across from hers opened and she turned to apologize for waking them, to find herself speechless.

Jason stood in his own doorway bare chested, in only a thin pair of pajama pants. His hair was mused and he looked a bit sleepy. Is this what it would have been like to wake up with him that morning, so long ago?

Her heart was pounding in her ears, her mouth went dry, and she curled both of her hands into fists to keep from reaching for him. How cruel was fate to bring him back into her life just to tease her with what she would never have?

Noticing her friend's difficulty, spoke up. "Sorry, she had a bit too much at girl's night."

He looked as if he were going to say something but looked Nicole over and he seemed to

changed his mind. "It's fine. I wasn't really sleeping."

She thought she heard Summer mutter, "Good." but couldn't be sure.

"Thanks, Summer, but I've got it from here."

Going into her room, she shut the door and leaned against it. It was going to be another long night.

Chapter Three

"So far you haven't shown me why you were worth searching for. Do better." Summer had tossed his way before exiting.

Since Jason was sure that she wasn't referring to his job, it made him think. Had Nicole been looking for him? And for how long, and when had she stopped? Was it a clue that she had never forgotten him?

If the way she had looked at him in the hallway was any indication she still found him attractive. Which was good to know since he found it increasingly difficult to keep a distance between them. The smell of her perfume haunted him as he walked through the house, and the sound of her voice drew his attention, no matter what he was doing. He'd never had anything distract him so easily.

His brother was right about one thing, he couldn't leave without knowing what they could have between them. He owed it to himself to find out.

Nicole had done a good job of avoiding him yesterday, except for dinner, but he knew where to find her right now and he wasted no time.

He made his way down the hall to where she spent Friday afternoons with T.J. working on reading for pleasure instead of research. He stopped just outside of the door and listened to them discuss what they had been reading, Harry Potter by the sounds of it.

The boy was the first to notice him. "Hey, Jason."

She looked up with questioning blue eyes. "Would you like to join us?"

"I was hoping to speak with you privately, but don't let me disturb you."

T.J. jumped up like a spring was released beneath him. "I'm going to check on the cookies." he said as he ran past.

Jason was surprised, but quickly took advantage and stepped in, shutting the door behind him. She was sitting on one of the comfortable chairs in the corner, and seemed to tense at the thought of being alone with him.

He took the chair that T.J. had vacated, adjacent from hers. "I wanted to apologize for the way I reacted. The truth is I have trouble dealing with strong emotions, especially when it's unexpected."

Her eyes widen as she replied, "I should be apologizing to you for the way I treated you then. You have every right to be angry."

"It wasn't just anger," he spoke softly. "It was disappointment."

"What?" she was clearly confused.

He shook his head. "It doesn't matter. My behavior was inexcusable."

"So, am I forgiven?"

"If you'll answer a question I've had since last night?"

"What question?"

"Your friend said something about you trying to find me." He watched her closely. "When was that?"

She licked her lips while she was thinking, and it distracted him for a moment. "It was the week before you got here. It's why I was late for lunch when you arrived."

He thought for moment about how she must have felt to arrive home to find him standing there, probably the same way he had. "I know how you felt. I have always hoped to see you again."

She didn't give any sign that the statement meant anything to her and asked, "Am I forgiven?"

"Of course." He smiled. "Why did you decide to try to find me?"

"I've been widowed for eight years now and everyone keeps telling me I need to get back out there. I ignored them until Mom and Rose came up with this scheme." waving her hand to indicate him.

"I'm part of a scheme?" he inquired.

"You mean that you haven't figured it out yet?" She smiled brightly. "The seating arrangements at dinner, your room practically across from mine, and the fact that it took them over a month to find someone for the position when they interviewed dozens of Male professors."

It dawned on him what she was saying. "I had been told that it was a difficult position to obtain and I was surprised when I got the call because I have little experience with either teaching or young children. It's because they're playing match maker?"

"Exactly." she agreed. "I don't want you to be caught off guard at anything they may suggest."

He pondered the new information. He was in house with people intent on matching him with the only woman he was interested in.

"T.J. seemed a little disappointed that he couldn't spend all of his summer to learning science." he commented.

"That's why we chose Harry Potter. I want him to know there's more to learn than science." she explained. "And it's our special time together."

"I believe the latter is what made him give in." he replied.

"Do you do any reading for pleasure?"

"I've read 'Around the world in 80 Days'. Someone suggested it once."

She smiled, remembering doing it as they strolled the decks of the ship, years ago. "Is that what made you want to travel?"

"Partly." He was uneasy with the question and changed the subject. "I remember that you wanted to travel. What happened?"

"I became a mother sooner than planned, not that I would change that, but it was out of the question then."

He gestured around them; to the rich furniture, paintings, and leather-bound books. "It seems that you had the money, surely your husband took you places."

Nicole looked away, toward the door and sighed, "Where is my son?"

Jason grinned. "My guess is he found the cookies."

She rose, obviously going to look for him. "He shouldn't have too many so close to dinner."

He rose as well. "Considering what you told me he's probably being kept away since the two of us are alone together."

Her smile returned as she resumed her seat. he followed suit. She didn't want to discuss her husband, and that was fine with him. When he thought of her with someone else, he saw red and wanted to do someone physical damage.

"So, instead of traveling, you opened a book store."

"Yes. Summer went to culinary school and wanted to start a bakery when the lady that formerly got all of that business retired, but didn't have enough money. We were talking and come up with the coffee shop/book store idea. She still makes most of her money on special occasion cakes. She's even had some orders from the city."

"Sounds like you two are doing well."

"It helps that I'm the only one that sells more than Christian Books. Not that it isn't a good thing but there are lessons to be learned from other works of literature." she tried to be modest. "Having the bakery does draw customs to the book store as well."

"Do you worry that T.J. won't be well rounded?"

"It worries me sometimes. I've seen some people with his brains with no personality and who don't seem to have any emotions. He also worries about the planet and the country."

He nodded. "I'm just thankful for my brothers. They made sure that I didn't stay buried in my studies. Dragging me out to play games and sports, whether I was good at them are not. But I was never chosen last when choosing teams."

"How may brothers do you have?"

"Two older and one younger. Glen is the oldest and a plumber with a wife and two daughters. Chad is next. He works for the electric company and he's married with a son and one on the way. Seth is the youngest and the one I'm closest with. He just retired from the Army and is trying to decide his next step."

"What about your parents?"

"My father is a brew master at Sweet Water Brewery." he told her, proudly. Then grew grim. "My mother took off after Seth's first week of school."

"Well, my mom finally kicked out my alcoholic father when I was twelve. We haven't heard anything since." Nicole informed him. "It killed her to do it but after so many years of false hope she gave up on tough love and sent him on his way. I sometimes wonder if she still loves him."

"No one knows why Mom left, but she was only seventeen when she met my father, ten years her senior, and got pregnant with Glen. We assume that she's out exploring the world, since she never got the chance, or that's what Seth thinks. My father doesn't discuss her."

"He still loves her." Nicole guessed.

He nodded. "I think the first few years he believed that she would be back, but gave up once we were all grown."

Apparently deciding the conversation could use a pick me up. Nicole asked him, "What kind
of trouble did four boys find to get into in the city?"

As he told her a funny story, he noticed that she still tilted her head to the right when she listened, and her laugh still touched his ears like a warm caress. Little had changed about her over the years and he became more certain of his decision. There was no one else now, and no reason for her to run away.

NICOLE DIDN'T REALIZE how long they had been talking until they were summoned to dinner by a grinning

Rose. She still wasn't sure how she'd kept from blushing as they all walked to the dining room together.

She had enjoyed hearing about his childhood with his brothers. Of course, she wasn't sure how they all managed to come out alive. She also felt bad for them growing up without a mother. They may have been boys raised by a good father, but all children needed a mother.

She was thankful every day for her mother, her rock. Knowing her mother was on her side, no matter the decision, had made her stronger. Watching her mother had taught her to be independent and to never accept less than you deserve. The latter is where Nicole could use some work.

They arrived to find Jean and T.J. already in their places and the meal set out. Jason held out Rose's chair as Nicole seated herself. It was a pleasant meal for her since there wasn't as much tension between the two of them. At least, not over anger of the past.

Occasionally their arms would brush and her mind would flash back to him in the hallway the night before. Her body reacted the same way now- her mouth grew dry, and her heart pounded in her ears.

She tried to concentrate on the conversation, but it was difficult, until Rose asked her a question that she didn't hear.

"I'm sorry. My mind slipped away for a moment." Nicole apologized.

"I was saying that it would be nice if you gave Jason a tour of town, introduce him to some people his own age." Rose repeated. "I'm sure he doesn't want to spend all of his time with a child and two old ladies."

"You two aren't old." Jason told her. "And I'm enjoying the company, but I wouldn't mind a tour."

Everyone turned to her, waiting for her answer. "It sounds great. We can go tomorrow. I'll call Summer and arrange to meet them for lunch at the diner."

They all looked surprised that she had agreed so readily. Honestly, she was as well. Nothing had changed between last night and now except that they could be friends. He'd shown no interest in anything else.".

It wasn't until they were all throwing out ideas of where she could take him that she realized she'd stepped into a trap. Shaking her head, she knew there was no backing out, even if she wanted to. The rest of the meal passed quickly as they described their favorite places in New Hope.

"Would you like to come T.J.?" She asked.

Shaking his head, he answered, "No, ma'am. I'm going to read some more."

"You know, I'm off tomorrow," Jean put in. "Why don't you have Summer drop her kids off here. I haven't seen them in a while."

"If you will excuse me, I'll go make the call."

Walking down the hall, she dug her cell from her pocket and wondered, again, what she had gotten herself into. She had thought T.J. would be happy to come along but he seemed to be in on the matchmaking as well.

Summer laughed after hearing the situation. "I thought they may be getting desperate."

"It's a good thing we had already talked things out." Nicole remarked.

"When did this happen?"

"This afternoon he found me and apologized for his behavior, that he realized he'd been more disappointed than angry. By the way, why did you tell him I'd been searching for him?"

"Because I knew you wouldn't." Summer told her, directly. "Besides, I didn't tell him. I just said that he hadn't shown me why you would try."

"Why would you say that?"

"Because David hurt you enough in that sham of a marriage and I'm not going to let that happen again. Neither will my husband for that matter."

"David may have humiliated me, but he didn't hurt me. I walked in with my eyes open."

"Are you telling me that you knew the entire time?"

"About Clair? Not until right before the wedding."

"Nic, that's taking the not breaking promises thing a little far."

"I was carrying his child and that child deserved to know who his father was. I'm not sure that would have happened if I'd broken things off."

"Damn it, Nicole. When are you going to worry about how your decisions affect you instead of how they affect everyone else?"

"I didn't call to talk about the past. It's over and can't be changed."

"At least I know I was right."

"About what?" Nicole asked, tiredly.

"Before you married David, I got the feeling that you were having second thoughts, but you never said anything so I didn't know for sure."

"You were right. My time away, and my time with Jason made me think."

"Are you going to tell Jason how you feel?"

"And how do I feel?"

"The way you looked at him last night made me think you were going have him right there." Summer told her.

She felt the flush creep up her cheeks. "He doesn't seem interested in more and it would be

complicated with him being T.J.'s mentor. What if things went wrong?"

"Excuses? I told you to think about yourself, for once."

"Like I said, he hasn't shown any interest in more than what we have now and I don't blame him. Just because he forgave me doesn't mean he'll forget."

"What if he does show interest?"

For a minute she let herself think about being in his arms again. Would it be the same as well? The same heat and passion. Dousing those thoughts, she told her friend, "I'll think about it if it happens."

Chapter Four

Jason found himself shadowed by T.J. when he left the dining room and headed out back to the garden. He sat on a stone bench, while the boy sat beside him.

"I get the feeling that you want to talk to me about something," he said.

The boy looked over at him. "Do you like my mom?"

"Of course, I like her." Jason replied. "I spent the afternoon talking to her."

"Do you want to kiss her?"

Jason smiled. "What do you know about kissing?"

"Aunt Summer and Uncle Charles. do it all the time," he made a face. "But Mom and Dad didn't. They never acted the way my aunt and uncle do."

Not sure how to reply to that he just said, "Some people aren't comfortable with public displays."

T.J. shook his head. "They didn't spend a lot of time together alone. Sometimes dad would leave after dinner and not come home until late."

"How do you know that?"

Shrugging, T.J. admitted, "I heard my grandparents talking about it. My grandmas worry that she's lonely now."

"What do you think?" Jason would never think of asking another child his age, but knew that T.J. would have an opinion.

"I think she was lonely then too."

Jason turned to the boy and made him meet his eyes. "I'm here for you. To be your tutor and mentor in the years to come. Whatever happens or doesn't happen with your mother will not change that."

The boy nodded, solemnly, then grinned, "I think you want to kiss her."

Jason chuckled. "You go inside and get ready for bed, Scamp. I'm sure they're searching for you."

Jason stood and watched as he went in the side door before heading deeper into the garden. He hadn't wanted to know about Nicole's husband, or marriage, but it seemed that it may be important if he wanted to win her.

He couldn't stop smiling when he thought of the boy's observations. He did indeed want to kiss Nicole. He'd thought about it the entire time they had been alone together. He'd watched her lips as she talked, wondering if she would taste the same. He wanted to take her in his arms more than he'd wanted anything in his life.

He wanted her to be the one to teach him about love, romantic love, just as he had years ago. Even having a taste of the pain that was to come if they parted hadn't changed his mind. He was about to step into the unknown, and he was nervous for the first time that he could remember.

His decision made he turned to head back inside when he saw her; she came from between the roses, dressed in a satin robe that although tide at the waist showed the lace of a matching gown. The moon was high in the sky, gleaming on her red and gold hair. She was so beautiful that, for a moment, he couldn't speak.

She beat him there though. "I spoke to Summer and we'll meet them in town at twelve thirty. They're both looking forward to meeting you.

He approached her slowly. "That sounds good." He stopped a step away from her. "When do we get started?"

Their gazes met and she licked her lips before answering. "Ten. That gives us time for breakfast."

He closed the distance between them and spoke softly. "I've been wondering about something all evening."

"What's that?" Her voice barely above a whisper.

Putting his hands on her hips he pulled her closer. He felt her slight shiver and inhale sharply. "This isn't a question you can answer with words."

She just nodded her accent as her body rose. He cupped her by the back of the neck and leaned down to meet her lips. They were soft and parted beneath his and she tasted of mint toothpaste.

He'd meant to keep his distance, a simple kiss to remind her of what they had once, but her strawberry scent ensnarled him. Her hands moved up his chest to grip the collar of his shirt, as if she was afraid that her legs would fail her. He found himself pulling her against his body and wrapping her fully in his arms.

When he felt as if he had to have her or stop, he released her and ended the kiss, knowing that if he didn't, he would take things too far and she would have regrets. She gave a sigh as she lowed back, flat on her feet.

She fiddled with the belt that held her robe tight for a minute before she inquired. "Did you get your answer."

She looked so cute standing there that he wanted to continue with what they had been doing.

Instead, he replied, "I think we both did." and headed inside.

NICOLE HAD GONE TO bed replaying that kiss in her mind over and over, which led to dreams so steamy she had no choice but to take a cold shower, again, before getting dressed. She couldn't help but thinking that he was right in that they both had an answer to the question.

She just didn't know what it meant for them. What was he looking for? What was she looking for? Shaking her head, she dressed in a short and tank set of yellow and went down to breakfast.

Everyone was already there, enjoying the breakfast of waffles with sausage and bacon. She took her seat next to Jason and began to help herself. From the corner of her eye, she gazed at him. He was dressed in a pair of cargo shorts of navy and white polo shirt.

Their hands met as they both reached for the syrup and he jerked away, but not before she left the tingle move from her hand up her arm.

"Ladies first." he told her.

She nodded and hurriedly added what she needed and set the bottle on the table between them. "Thank you."

She caught her mother and Rose exchange a secret smile, but said nothing as they reminded her of the places they should stop. Meanwhile, she felt as if she got an electric shock every time their arms brushed and wondered why she hadn't noticed it before. Maybe because they had both been careful not to touch until the night before. The thought made her grow warm and she wondered how she was going to last the day with him.

After eating, as they were leaving Nicole turned to remind them, "We have lunch plans but we *will* be back for dinner."

Once at her car he opened the driver door for her. "My lady." he joked.

"Why thank you. Men don't open doors anymore."

He got in the passenger side before commenting, "That's because most women take it as some sort of insult. My father taught us that a gentleman always opens a door for a lady, and if she doesn't appreciate it, she's not a true lady, just another woman of the world."

"He sounds like a good man." She pulled out of the drive and began the tour. "He raised you all well, being a single father."

"Why is it assumed that men will do worse as a single parent than a woman?"

"I didn't mean anything by it. My cousin, Brittany, was raised by a single father. Of course, a girl goes through things a boy doesn't."

"Ahh, I see what you're saying. Yes, I believe he dealt with issues my father is glad he didn't have to address."

As they made their way around, she pointed out several things, stopping several times, the longest at the place they done the archaeological dig the year before. It was roped off but that didn't stop Jason from going over the rope to look into the giant hole, that was actually the opening to a tunnel.

He looked at her in surprise. "Is this really a part of the underground railroad?"

She smiled at his reaction. "Some kids were playing here and one fell into a covered whole that the board had rotted through. They uncovered several items and called the scientists in. Dr, Spade was a good man and allowed T.J. to help with the work. He was taught how to dig properly for artifacts, helped to store and label them."

"He talked about it but I don't think that I believed him." Jason admitted.

"The town is still trying to decide what to do with the property, to draw some tourism."

"I wish I could go down." Jason replied.

"You will have to make do with the pictures I have put in an album for T.J." she told him. She pointed to the top of the post around the area. "They have cameras to keep the kids away."

"So, there would be no point in calling for reinforcements to help." Jason teased.

"I think that would cause a lot more trouble than your brothers want at our age."

He walked back toward her, stopping just a few inches away. "I suppose you're right." he agreed, brushing a stray lock of hair behind her ear.

She tried to hide the shiver by stepping back and walking back to the car. The next stop was of her choosing. She wanted to share a few stories of her teen years, so she drove them to the high school.

The parking lot was empty, except for a couple of cars that were over by the football field. When they got out, she could hear the band practicing as well. She met him in front of where she had parked.

"This is the local high school." she informed him. "It hasn't changed much since I went here."

"What were you like then?" he asked.

"I was a serious student, trying to earn academic scholarship." she answered. "I worked part time during the Summer, to save money for any extras I may need for higher education. Summer and Charles got me to a few parties, but I' would have rather been home reading than watching sloppy drunks."

His deep chuckle rang through the air. "We had that in common."

"I was also on the yearbook staff and the school newspaper."

"Did you ever do anything to get in trouble?" he asked as they walked along the sidewalk, near the football field.

She felt heat on her cheeks and knew that she was blushing. She stepped off of the grass and

led him to the fence.

"You can't get in trouble if you're never caught." she teased. He smiled over at her and she continued, "The one high school tradition that has lasted since the seventies is the Senior Prank. Charles, Summer, and I stole the principles car. We drove it here and parked it on the fifty-yard line and covered it with post its."

He chuckled again. "But you were never caught."

She shook her head. "It was the best prank of the year and we never took credit for it."

"You see that's where our situations would have been different. My brothers wouldn't have been able to resist bragging." he remarked, then spoke softly. "Thank you."

She turned her head to look at him. "For what?'

He reached over to put a loose strand of hair behind her ear, "For sharing a part of yourself with me."

"You're welcome." she stepped back. "We should head on ever to the diner."

She hadn't been sure why she had wanted to come here. Perhaps it had been a way of showing him a part of her life. She knew they would never be what she had hoped when she'd been looking for him. He'd seen the worst side of her, and she couldn't blame him, but they could be friends.

THEY PARKED IN FRONT of a diner, and Jason assumed they would be eating there. He'd been enjoying being in Nicole's company, though she seemed a little nervous. He hoped it was because of the way he'd found reasons to touch her.

He couldn't help himself. The sun glittered off her red braid and the yellow shorts showed her shapely legs. As they walked side by side, he noticed every time they hand's brushed, she would blush, lightly.

"This is our downtown square." she was saying. "It may not look like much but we're proud of it." she continued to tell him about the town history until they stopped in the park to look at the Memorial Wall of vets.

"Do you have family on here?"

"I think everybody in town has a family member's name up there. My grandfather was in Vietnam." She walked over and pointed out the name. Then she spotted someone and grinned. "You're in luck. You're about to meet one of our town eccentrics."

She took him by the hand and led him to a bench where an African American lady sat with a bright pink purse and matching hat. As they drew closer, he saw that it was actually a man dressed as a woman in a white Sunday dress.

She looked up and greeted Nicole with a bright smile. "It's good to see you out for fun. It's about time." Then she turned and looked Jason over. "Who is your tall, dark, and handsome friend?"

"Rhonda, this is T.J.'s tutor, Dr. Jason Matthews." Nicole introduced him. "Jason, this is Rhonda."

Rhonda glanced to where their hands were still joined between them. "Taking advantage of his presence, are you?"

Nicole dropped his hand and blushed bright red. "I was just bringing him over to meet you."

Rhonda laughed and they discussed T.J. and what he was learning. Then, glancing at her watch she stood

"I'm sorry to rush off but I have a hair appointment." Rhonda gave him one more look, slapped his ass, and rushed away.

He was still getting over the slap when he heard Nicole giggle at his side. He looked at her accusingly. "You could have warned me."

Shaking her head, she responded, "And miss that shocked look? It what she lives for. Does it to visitors all of the time."

When they headed back toward the diner, she explained why Rhonda was a legend in their small town.

"She was the first to openly live her life the way she felt inside. In her twenties she came out and stood strong against everyone who claimed there was something wrong with her. The young people in town that feel the same way, look at all she's been through and know that they can do the same if they have the courage."

"I have a feeling that she was someone you have look to for courage as well."

"Yes." was all she said and they reached their destination.

He opened the door for her and almost ran into her back when she froze just inside the doorway. She was staring at a waitress with blond hair.

He touched her lightly on the arm. "Is everything alright?"

She nodded and replied, "Summer and Charles are in the corner."

He followed her and slid in the booth after her. While she made the introductions, he noted that the couple seemed uneasy.

But Summer cleared that up when she spoke, "I'm sorry, Nikki, we didn't know she was here until we were seated, but we can go somewhere else."

"No reason for that." Nicole said, "And nothing to apologize for. I was going to run into her sooner or later,"

Jason made a mental note to find out what it was about as he picked up is menu. The other couple was nice and accepting and he wondered how much they knew about him. He knew they were the ones they were with on the cruise so they may know more than her family.

"It sounds as though you have been a threesome for a while." he commented.

"We grew up within a mile of each other on the same dirt road." Charles said. "Grew up riding bicycles back and forth."

Summer shared a secret smile with her husband before speaking, "Even after Charles and I realized we were more than fiends, we never left her out. Well, we did take time as a coupe."

"Time I was happy to give you." Nicole squeezed her friend's hand on the table. "I needed time to study anyway."

He caught Summer looking at him a couple of times and wondered what was on her mind. When they finished Summer and Nicole excused themselves, leaving the two men alone.

Charles turned serious as soon as they were out of earshot. "What are your intentions toward Nicole?"

"I'm not sure what you mean."

"You know that Nicole is a special person, and we would hate to see her hurt again." Charles replied.

"What do you mean, again? I wasn't aware that I had hurt her." Jason asked.

"Not you. David." Charles said. "What do you know about her marriage?"

"Not much." He didn't feel he should share what T.J. had told him. "Why do you ask? What was he like?"

"He was your typical rich kid, jock, and the girls loved him." Charles glanced in the direction the ladies had gone before continuing, "We don't have much time so I'm going to tell you the story quick. Nicole was the girl in high school that seemed untouchable; beautiful, smart, an no one ever had a bad word to say about her. She dated but never seriously, usually as a group. It became a competition to see who could get her virginity. That's what caught David's attention, and the fact that she didn't seem to know he was alive only made him try harder. Everyone knew that he had no real interest in strait laced girl, like our Nicole."

Jason cut in to ask. "What kind of girls were his type?"

Jutting his chin in the direction of one of the waitresses. "Clair is my cousin and they were involved until the day he died."

Jason looked over at the one they were talking about. Her skirt was too short and her shirt was so small it seemed that her large breast would burst out at any moment. Then he realized what the other man was saying. "You mean that he was having an affair?"

Charles nodded. "And it wasn't a secret. Her parents disowned her and she moved to the city. David would go see her every night before heading home."

"Why would she stay with him?"

"We always assumed that she didn't know until close to the end, but it turns out she knew the entire time. I'm not sure why she stayed. Of course, no one ever understood why she went out with him in the first place." The other man shook his head. "I think she done it out of respect for his folks. She swore that she would never cause pain to those she loved, and she loves Rose and Tom Sr."

"She never thought of doing the same?"

"I don't think so. Since being widowed she's only gone out a hand full of times, and that was because everyone pushed her." Charles starred at him a moment before adding, "You are the only man she's ever shown interest in, and that includes David. What he did hurt her pride and humiliated her, but he could never hurt her.

"My wife believes that Nicole never loved him, she cared for him, but never loved." he watched Jason's reaction. "Now can you understand our concern? He couldn't hurt her, but I think that you could. So, what are your intensions?"

Jason was thinking over what he'd learned and trying to formulate an answer when Clair stopped at their table.

"Hey, cousin, why don't you introduce me to your handsome friend.?" She spoke to Charles but her eyes were racking over Jason.

"Clair, we specifically asked not to be in your section. I think you understand why."

Clair ignored him. And smiled at Jason, "I'm Clair. How long have you been in town?"

Jason took a closer look at the woman David had chosen over his wife and wondered if the man had been insane. She was a gorgeous woman with her curled blond hair, and curves that she obviously loved to show off. But her eyes seemed empty, as if devoid of thoughts and dreams of her own.

He was saved from conversing with her by Summer and Nicole's arrival back at the table.

Chapter Five

Summer turned on Nicole as soon as the door shut behind them. "What's going on with you? I've never seen you so fidgety before."

She shouldn't be surprised. Her best friend knew her better than anyone. "He kissed me last night in the garden."

Summer grinned at her. "And you said he wasn't interested."

"He didn't show any when we spent the afternoon talking, but last night he waited for me to take my stroll in the garden. He said he had a question that needed answering and he kissed me."

"And did he get his answer?" Summer was smirking now.

"When I asked, he said that we both did." Nicole dug the lip gloss from her purse. "I got an answer alright, but did he come to the same conclusion?"

The other woman brushed her blond hair. "What was yours?"

"Yes."

Their gazes met in the mirror. "To what?"

She thought again of being held by him, his kisses warming her blood, and the heat pooling low in her stomach. She sighed, "Anything."

Summer laughed so loud Nicole wouldn't be surprised if the whole diner heard her, and felt herself blush. She knew how much yearning had come out in that one word.

Summer caught her breath. "What are you going to do about it?"

Closing her purse with a snap, she responded, "I don't know. He's signed up to be in T.J.'s life for a long time and if things didn't work out between us...There's more to consider now."

Summer shook her head and tsked. "You, my friend, are the queen of excuses." Then she washed her hands. "All I'm saying is you better snap him up before someone else does."

They were giggling when they exited the restroom and Nicole stopped in her tracks again. Standing next to their table was Clair, her late husband's mistress, flirting with Jason.

She felt herself begin to shake with an urge she'd never felt before- to do someone physical harm.

She couldn't tell if he was responding, but it didn't matter. She had kept quiet all of those years because she didn't care. If the bitch thinks that was still the case, she was about to find out differently.

She heard Summer say her name lowly, as she stalked over to where they had left the men. Stopping beside the waitress she smiled, "Hello, Clair, I'm sorry but we won't need anything else."

Clair narrowed her eyes, "I'm just getting off and stopped to talk to my cousin I haven't seen in years."

She laid her hand om Jason's shoulder. "Well, don't let us stop you. We have one more stop to make before we go back to the mansion."

She heard several people in tables close by gasp, and saw Summer laughing behind her hand as Clair's mouth dropped open. But the lady didn't move so that Jason could rise.

"Sorry, was I too polite. Skank Patrol, step to the side." She ordered, as nastily as she could.

Clair's mouth snapped shut, and she stalked away. The whispers began as Jason got to his feet, and grew louder the closer they got to the door. Her steam carried her until she got in the car, then she began to feel ashamed of herself.

There was every chance that Jason liked what he saw in Clair, most men did. With her curvy body and made-up face. She owed him an apology.

She turned toward him in the passenger seat to find him smiling at her. She went on anyway, "I'm sorry. I'm not usually petty but when I saw her talking to you... I don't know what come over me." She moved to start the car.

He put his over the hand she had holding the keys and stopped her. "You should know that Charles explained to me, about her. He wouldn't have except that I noticed your reaction and I ask. I think he wanted me to get the truth instead of rumors."

She felt the flush that heated her cheeks and thought how he must see her now. As some housewife that couldn't keep her own husband interested on their marriage bed. She stared straight ahead, not wanting to see the pity in his eyes, that she saw when she'd looked at so many others.

She felt his fingers caress her cheek, and he whispered. "I think he must have been insane." Surprised to feel his breath on her cheek, she turned to face him. The tips of their noses touched. "And we were trying to get rid of her anyway."

"R,,,really?"

He nodded. "Although, I wasn't aware we were making another stop."

Taking a deep breath, she explained, "I thought I would show the house that I grew up in."

"Showing me another part of yourself." So low she almost didn't hear him, then he remarked as he sat back. "Can I see your childhood bedroom? Is it covered in posters of rock stars?"

"No rock stars." she told him, but couldn't keep from giggling as she started the car.

"I enjoyed getting to see you around your friends. You're different with them than with your family." he commented.

"I love Rose like my own mother and I have always been grateful for the way she and her husband accepted me. I don't want to ever do anything to make her think less of me." She tried to explain. "And Charles and Summer made it clear that I didn't have to play the grieving widow with them."

"Did you love your husband?" he asked, sounding timid.

"I cared for him, and without him I wouldn't have T.J. but I'm not sure about love." she found herself telling him. "I'm not sure I was ever looking for love. I never even pictured myself married, but I got caught up in small town expectations."

"What expectations?"

"Women can have dreams and a career, but she's still expected to settle down, marry, and have children." she found herself confiding. "It wasn't the children that I questioned, but the marriage. I heard my mother cry for months after she finally got tired of my father's drinking and kicked him out. Before that were the fights." she shrugged. "It was better once he was gone."

Jason got quiet. She couldn't see his expression, since her eyes were on the road, and wondered what he was thinking. Then he spoke, "It was different with my mother. She and dad were in love, hardly ever argued, then one day she was gone."

"Does anyone know why she left?"

"Just theories." Then he looked around. "This is the opposite side of town than where you live now."

She nodded. "We're not as well-off as they are."

"I did notice that your mother works." he replied. "I just thought she loved the work as a nurse."

"She does but it's also to keep the bills paid at the house I'm about to show you. She only moved in after the accident to help with things. She's threatened to move back but I believe she hates the thought of being alone again." She made the turn onto a dirt road. "She insists on paying Rose rent. The argued for weeks until a compromise was made."

"This should be interesting."

"Rose stopped arguing and complaining, and Mom didn't understand why. Rose had taken the money and started a savings account for T.J. When Mom found out and objected Rose told her that the money was hers to do with as she pleased, and that's what pleased her. That way Mom pays rent but Rose feels she's not taking advantage for all that mom does at the house."

Jason chuckled. "I'm just glad all T.J. remembers is the happy times."

"He may remember more than you think." Jason informed her. "Children with his IQ tend to hold memories longer."

"I didn't realize. Has he said something to you?"

"If he, had I wouldn't feel comfortable sharing."

She nodded. She understood but it also didn't answer her question. "Just promise me that if there's something harming him you will let me know."

He reached over and let his finger glide down her arm her arm, causing her to shiver, "Of course."

She pulled into the yard that she'd walked across every day, until she got married. Nothing had changed. The house still stood proudly in the yard with rose bushes all the way around. The swung on the front porch, that looked as if it had been repainted.

He walked around the car and opened to door for her. "I haven't been by in a while, although Mom comes by to check on things regularly." She led him around back, where the remnants of a ball field remained. "This is where we played ball and out in the trees, there." she pointed to the trees in the distance. "Is where we had our shaving cream and water balloon fights."

"Why both? He wondered aloud.

"The water balloons were Mom's idea, after the first time we came in covered on shaving cream."

"The water washed away the shaving cream." he concluded.

She grinned and nodded at him. Then turned her face to him. "Would you like to see the inside?"

His eyes shone with mischief, "You did promise I could see your room."

She laughed. "I don't recall promising."

He gave her a sexy smile. "I want to see what kind of posters are on your walls."

As she led him back to the front door, she wondered what had come over her to bring him here. She had considered it over lunch but hadn't made a decision until she'd come out to see Clair talking to him. She'd never felt such a rush of anger as she had in that moment.

Unlocking the door, they stepped inside. He walked around her to look at the living room, with its view of the kitchen.

"Your Mom afforded this on a nurse's salary?" he asked.

Glad to have something else to think about, she explained, "This has been in the family for generations. It started as two rooms with a loft. My great, great, great, you get the picture, grandfather. When he proposed, all he had was the money saved to buy the land and he refused to marry until he built the house. Every generation has added to it until it became what you see today."

He turned and walked over to her. "That's a romantic story."

She met his brown eyes and lost her breath. The clear grey had darkened like a sudden storm. She'd seen then that color only once before and she was as shaken now as she had been then.

"I... I shouldn't have brought you here." she stuttered.

He cupper her face with one hand and stroked her cheek with his thumb, "Why not? Because we're alone in a place where no one will find us."

"Yes." she answered, honestly.

His other hand went to her waist, to pull her closer. "I've thought of this moment since I saw you again."

Before she could respond he leaned down and covered her mouth with his. This kiss was different from the night before. It wasn't questioning, it was possessive, and filled with desire that she responded to automatically. Her hands slid up his chest, filling his muscles tense beneath them, and gripped his shoulders as she pressed herself closer.

At that sign of her acceptance one hand went to the back of her neck to hold her steady as the other wrapped around her waist and lifted her slightly off the ground. The kiss deepened as her hands found their way around his neck and into his hair. The wavy locks were soft to the touch and he smelled of fresh air and cloves.

Then she felt he wall at her back as one of his hands gripped one of her thighs, and the other slid around to cup her breast. She felt them swell to fill his hands and her nipples hardened.

Breaking the kiss to catch her breath and try to grab a hold of some restrain didn't work since his lips and tongue drifted down her exposed neck. She felt his erection through his shorts and rubbed herself against it in a move to ease her own ache.

When he lifted his head, he was breathing as heavily as she was. "Tell me to stop or direct me to the nearest room before I take you right here."

He was putting the choice in her hands, not taking it from her with desire, and her heart skipped a beat. There was only one decision, "Down the hall, last door to the left."

He lifted her so that her legs wrapped around his waist and her arms around his neck. He resumed kissing her hungrily as he rushed to the room she'd indicated. He set her on her feet as their hands ran over each other's bodies, heatedly, removing clothing with a speed, she was surprised she didn't hear ripping.

He then backed her toward the bed where they fell together; she on her back and him coming to rest on at her side.

His hands continued over her hips and thighs as his lips found her breasts.

As he licked and nipped each one, she ran her hands through his hair, over his shoulders and back. His hands glided over her body followed by flames heated her flesh.

Her body responded to him automatically, letting him touch her in areas no one but she had touched in years. She was wet and welcoming as he entered her, and her legs wrapped around his waist as their bodies became reacquainted with each other. It was better than her memories and dreams put together.

The orgasm hit her so fast that all she could do was wrap herself tighter around him as her body convulsed with pleasure. Him pulling out and emptying on her stomach and kissing her softly was the last thing she remembered before falling asleep.

After Nicole fell asleep, Jason held her in his arms as he glanced around the room. The bed was an antique metal canopy bed, painted white to match the dresser. There weren't rock posters on the wall, but posters celebrating literary works. Although there had been none on the bed, there were stuffed animals in a net, in the corner of the room. Underneath was a collage of pictures that he assumed were of her friends. He wasn't sure what he had expected, but it suited her.

Then he looked back at the woman he held. Her hair was mused and her lips swollen from his kisses. He had decided after their encounter in the garden that he would seduce her, but hadn't expected it to be so easy. He couldn't help but wonder if it was another way of her proving something to someone. The question was what and who.

She was sleeping so soundly, that he let her do so while he tried to think through the situation. He knew that she had tried looking for him, as he had looked for her for years, but what did it mean? Did she have feelings for him, or just looking for a little pleasure after being alone for so long.

He knew the later was true, because of the way she had turned fidgety when he brushed against her. She had seemed so shy and uncertain until she had confronted Clair. If that's what had given her the courage to allow this to happen, he would thank the other woman some time.

He decided then that she'd opened this door willingly and he wasn't going to let her close him out again. He still had no idea what his next move should be, but it was getting late in the afternoon and they had promised to be back for the evening meal.

She was laying spooned along the front of him, with her head pillowed on his arm. With his free hand he brushed her hair away from her neck and settled his lips there. When she only sighed his lips moved up to her delicate ear.

"Time to wake up, Sleeping Beauty." he whispered.

She looked around before turning in his arms. Not meeting his eyes, she asked, "How long was I out?"

"About an hour," he answered. He lifted her chin so that she was looking at him. "Do you regret what happened?"

Her eyes widened, "Of course not."

"What's wrong, then?"

Her eyes moved to his chest, where her hand lay over his heart. "I just know that my body isn't the same as before. I've gained weight and...."

He stopped whatever she was saying by kissing her breathless. "Your body is perfect. The only changes coming from giving birth, and that's beautiful."

"Not all men feel that way." she murmured.

"You must not have noticed the dirty looks I was getting from the local men at lunch."

She was running her fingers through the light covering of hair on his chest. "But they've never seen me like this."

He put his hand over her roaming one to stop it. "Please, tell me your husband never said anything negative about the changes in your body." When she rolled over to get up, he had his answer. "How big of a fool was this guy?"

Putting on her shirt she replied, "Of course he never said anything."

"But that's when you started sleeping in separate rooms?" he countered.

She turned to face him with a look of horror. "How did you know about that?"

"Does it matter? I see it as a sign of his stupidity, not your desirability."

He got up and pulled his shorts back on. What he didn't say was bubbling beneath the surface and he didn't want to say anything to make her think he was angry at her. If it were possible, he would bring David back from the dead, just to beat the hell out of him.

Walking around the bed he stood behind her, where she stood in front of the dresser mirror working on her hair. He wrapped an arm around her waist and pulled her back against him. "Your husband was a fool and you shouldn't let his choices shape who you are."

He saw the tears pool in her eyes before she spoke softly, "It doesn't matter."

He turned her in his arms and caught the tears in a kiss as they fell. Then he just held her against him until he felt she'd gotten control of herself.

"You make me feel like the most beautiful woman alive," she told him, then she pushed him away playfully. "I need to finish my hair if we don't want to be late."

"Do you think they'll suspect what happened?" he inquired, as he finished dressing.

That caused her to giggle. "Probably, but they won't say anything."

After straightening things up they headed out to the car, but he stopped her. She looked at him questioningly.

"Would you like to go on a date with me? We could have dinner in the city if you don't want people talking too much."

"I would love to." Then she laughed. "After the scene at the diner they will be talking about me either way. We can go wherever you like."

Nodding he told her, "I'll make arrangements and let you know."

Chapter Six

Nicole was glad to see that she was right when they had arrived back home. Other than a couple of knowing smiles sent her way, no one acted as if anything were different. They both went to their separate rooms to get ready for dinner.

The conversation centered on preparations for the Fourth of July holiday. Although she was barely listening. She was wondering what this afternoon meant for them. What did he expect from her?

He'd been tender with her when she'd been self-cautious of the changes in her body, but that didn't mean that he had feelings for her. He would have done the same for any woman he might have been with, he was a kind person.

Of course, she may need to examine what she wanted from him. She hadn't expected the events of the afternoon but she didn't regret them. Not even standing up to Clair, something Summer would have encouraged her to do long ago. She knew that it would cause gossip. It probably started before they had exited the diner door, and found that she didn't care.

She was so surprised by her thought she almost chocked on her broccoli. After s sip of water, she noticed that everyone was watching her.

"What did I miss?" she asked.

T.J. covered his giggle with his hand as Rose repeated her question. "Wouldn't it be nice if Jason invited his family to stay with us for the holiday?"

"Oh, yes. Defiantly." She turned to them. "You know that we have the room."

Jason nodded. "I'll talk to them."

"Good." Rose replied.

She felt the touch of Jason's hand on hers under the table and looked his way. Noting his look of concern, she gave him a small smile before sliding her hand away and using it to take a drink.

After dessert, she excused herself and went to her room. Removing her clothes, she stood in front of her full-length mirror and looked herself over. She hadn't realized before today that David's affair and moving out of their bedroom had affected the way she viewed herself.

Her body looked the same to her; well-rounded breasts and curved hips, shapely legs. They only problem area was the no longer flat abs. Funny how that one area could affect the way you see yourself. She smiled when she thought that Jason hadn't seemed to mind it at all.

Just as she slipped her night gown over her head her cell phone rang. She smiled when she saw her closest friends name pop up.

"Hello, Summer."

"Don't hello me. I've been waiting all afternoon for you to call."

Nicole decided to tease her a bit. "Whatever for?"

"You can start by telling me about that scene in the diner." Summer retorted. "Bravo, by the way. It's about time you stood up to her."

Just thinking about what she'd done embarrassed her now. "I don't know what got into me. I saw her and felt intense rage. It makes no sense. I've seen her around before, even caught sight if her with David once, and never felt that angry."

"It's called jealousy." Summer informed her. "You saw her flirting with the man you're interested in and you acted like any other woman would have."

"Why didn't I feel that way about her and my husband?" she asked herself more than Summer.

"You're the only one that can answer that." Her friend answered anyway. "So, where did you take him?"

"I took him to my old house and showed him where we had all the adventures that we were telling him about." She tried to sound nonchalant, but she knew it wouldn't fool Summer.

"OH, did you show him the inside?"

"Mostly the living room. Although we spent most of the time in my bedroom."

"I knew it." She could see her friend's grin in her mind. "How was it?"

Just remembering made her grow warm. "It was just as I remembered."

"So, what's going to happen now?"

"We haven't discussed it, but we're going to dinner in the city." Then she asked the question she had been putting off. "I suppose everyone was talking after we departed."

"Yes, but mostly cheering and clapping of hands." Summer told her. "No one blames you

for finally saying something to her. But you may want to watch your back, Clair was pissed."

"I don't care." Nicole told her. "There's nothing more she can do."

"But we both know that she'll try."

JASON WATCHED NICOLE leave the dining room before turning back to the rest of them. The ladies looked concerned.

"Did something happen to upset her while you were out?" her mother asked him.

"We ran into someone at the diner that upset her." he explained. "One of the waitresses."

Jean exchanged a look with Rose before getting T.J. from the room.

With a deep sigh Rose set her fork down. "I had heard that Clair had come back to town and made peace with her parents. Apparently, she spent everything David managed to leave her." She looked his way. "Did anyone explain to you?"

Jason nodded. "I got the story from Charles when the ladies were washing up."

She surprised him by saying what he'd been thinking all day. "My son was a damned fool."

"I have to admit that I don't understand the choice myself. Why he wanted Clair when he had Nicole waiting at home is beyond understanding."

"I assume she introduced herself." Rose commented. "Charles wouldn't have, cousin or not."

He told her the entire story, hoping that she wouldn't be angry with her daughter in law.

Rose grinned. "Well, well. Good for her."

"I think she regrets it because you will be embarrassed or angry with her." he confided.

"I'll talk to her about it." Rose assured him. "I wonder what could have finally pushed her over the edge?" But the look in her eye said that she already knew. "So, you can't see what my son saw I in his mistress."

This conversation had just taken a turn he hadn't counted on, but saw no reason not to be honest. "Nicole is beautiful, smart, and kind. Clair couldn't hold a candle to her.

"She doesn't see herself clearly." Rose replied. "I'm afraid my son hurt her in ways that she doesn't want to admit to herself. She's been alone longer than she's been a widow."

"Why did she stay?" he surprised himself by asking.

"I was never sure if it was for us or T.J." Rose said. "Thomas and I loved her from the start and tried to get David to do better by her. But he was obsessed with that blond bimbo, and rebelling against his father."

"We'll never know why he did what he did. All we can do is try to help her get past it." he spoke, softly.

"We? Are you a part of this now?"

He just smiled. "If you will excuse me, I'm going retire to my room."

He heard her soft laughter as he exited the room and headed toward the stairs, and found T.J. sitting at the bottom. He stood when he saw Jason and smiled.

"What's on your mind?' he asked as they headed up the stairs.

"Did you kiss her?" T.J. inquired.

He couldn't help but laugh at his straight forwardness. "You do realize there's more to adult relationships than kissing, don't you?"

The boy nodded. "The sleep together at night."

"T.J., your mom and I are trying to get to know each other, that's all you need to know for now."

They had reached the second floor by then and T.J. giggled before saying, "Yeah, you kissed her."

Jason tousled his black hair. "Is that why you waited on me? For guy talk?"

"Sort of." T.J. seemed nervous now. "Do you know how to play baseball?"

"I have four brothers, of course I can play. I'm not the best."

The boy's shoulders slumped. "Oh."

Jason stopped the boy and knelt down to his height. "What's wrong?"

"We always play with Aunt Summer's family over the holiday, but I can't hit the ball." T.J explained. "I thought if we could practice, I might get to surprise them this year."

"I see. Well, my younger brother was the captain of the team in high school, and was very good. What if I see if he can come a few days early and coach you?"

T.J. jumped up and down with excitement before running ahead to his mother's room. Without knocking he burst through the door. "Momma, guess what? Jason is going to ask his

brother to help me learn to hit."

Jason leaned against the doorway, watching and listening.

Nicole hugged her son. "That's great. But you could have asked Uncle Charles."

T.J. pulled out of her arms. "I know but he's not my dad. I know that Jason isn't either but this way I can surprise them at the game."

"I see." Ncole kissed his forehead. "But I believe that you're supposed to be in bed."

"I only stayed up to talk to Jason." he replied, heading toward the door. "Good night."

Nicole followed to her doorway and watched her son enter his room and shut the door. She was dressed for bed as well, in her ivory silk robe. She turned to him with a sweet smile. "That's kind of you, but are you sure that your brother will be willing."

"He's just retired his Army commission and hasn't decided his next step yet." he explained. "I'm sure that he'll enjoy some extra time away from the city."

"If Rose learns that she'll make him the guest of honor." she informed. "I'm sure he would rather avoid that attention."

"Let's not mention it then." he said. "Or leave it to him."

Her hair was damp, and sticking to her flushed cheek. Her reached to wipe it away but she beat him to it.

"Just let us know when they will arrive and we'll make sure we're ready for the extra guests."

He nodded and took one of her hands in his. "Would you like to walk through the garden?"

She gently slid her hand out of his, just as she had at dinner. "Another time. It's been a long day."

He straightened to stand. "Of course. Good night."

"Good night." she returned, before shutting the door.

As he went into his own room, he tried to tell himself that she was tired, had fallen asleep in his arms, but he couldn't convince himself. She had been acting differently from the time they had begun to drive home.

At the time he considered that she was worried about the gossip, even if she'd said she didn't care at the time. She cared about the way people saw her, that wouldn't change overnight. Now he was beginning to wonder if she regretted what had happened between them.

Before he drove himself crazy trying to figure her out, he pulled out his cell phone to keep his promise to T.J., and called Seth.

"Hey, Big Bro," Seth answered. "What's the news?"

"I'm calling for a favor." He filled him in on the barbeque for the fourth and the invitations for his family to join them. And T.J. requesting a coach. "So, do you have anything going on."

"I don't." Seth admitted. "But the two oldest booked a trip to Disney for their families six months ago."

"Well, let's not disappoint our nieces and nephews." he remarked. "You think Dad will come? Rose is looking forward to meeting a brew master."

"Any chance he gets to talk about work, he takes." Seth remarked. "You can count on the two of us. I'll have the kid hitting like it's second nature."

"That's what you said about me."

"Some people are hopeless." Was his brother's reply. "I'll talk to Dad and get back to you."

"Maybe I should talk to him." Jason said. "It may go easier."

"By all means, take the pressure off of me." Their father had always been hardest on Seth. None of them understood why, but Seth seemed to take it all in stride. "How are things otherwise?"

"I'm not sure." he admitted. "I thought things were progressing, but now I'm not so sure."

"Tell me about it and we'll figure it out."

So, he told his brother everything that had happened in the last forty-eight hours, sparing the obvious details. "Everything seemed fine. I realize that her marriage left her with some scars, but I was making progress with easing them."

"From what you've told me she's just beginning to realize that herself. Give her some time to adjust."

"I'll do that." he said, but he wasn't sure that was why she pulled away from his slightest touch sense they had been back here. "You should really go to school and take some phycology courses."

"I've been thinking about it."

Jason couldn't have been more surprised. "What changed your mind?"

"Visiting some friends that aren't doing as well as I am and wanting to be able to help." Seth remarked. "Most war wounds aren't physical."

"Good. I'll call dad tomorrow. Thanks for the advice."

"Any time."

Setting his cell on the bedside table, he got ready for a shower. He was disappointed that his older brothers wouldn't be here to meet everyone, but maybe he could arrange for them to meet Nicole while on their date.

IN THE PAST WEEK EVERYTHING had been almost perfect. She had shared lunch with Jason several times, as well as taking an afternoon off to join him and T.J. for fishing and a picnic. They had been disappointed that Jason's entire family couldn't make it but they were already preparing for Seth's arrival in a couple of weeks.

She'd heard some of the talk about her, but it wasn't too bad. Mostly, it didn't upset Rose, which was her primary concern. The woman couldn't help how her son lived and shouldn't bare the shame of it.

The older woman had given her a warm hug and assured her that she approved of her finally speaking up for herself and that she knew Nicole hadn't married David or stayed for the money.

Now it was Saturday afternoon and she was getting ready to ride with Jason into the city. He hadn't told her exactly what they would be doing but to dress casually. She finally settled on a powder blue sundress that cinched around her waist before falling to her knees. Since he was so tall, she also wore a matching pair of sandles with heels.

She was standing in front of the mirror, working on her hair when her mother knocked, then entered. "You look nice."

"Thanks." Her mother's forehead was crinkled with worry. "Is something wrong?"

"No." Jean sat on her bed. "I'm just curious about something."

Turning away from the mirror she joined her mother on the bed. "About what?"

With a small smile Jean began, "You know what Rose and I were up to with this tutor."

Nicole giggled. "Yes, I caught on pretty quickly."

"We worried that we had made a mistake the first week. It was obvious that you two had a disagreement right away. We couldn't understand it. She still doesn't."

"Do you?"

"I think that I've finally put it together." Jean confessed. "He's the one from the cruise, isn't he?"

Nicole couldn't believe what she was hearing. "How did you know that?"

"It was the way he first looked at you, as if he'd found something he'd been looking for. I thought he was struck by how beautiful you were and fell instantly in love. When he followed you to the store and came back upset, it was pretty clear that you had argued. I remember that you said you left before he had woken and figured he was angry."

"Very angry." Nicole confirmed. "When I walked in and saw him I almost fainted. We did argue, but we talked things out last week."

Jean laughed, "That's one way to put it."

"Rose doesn't know, does she?" Nicole asked, suddenly afraid of what the older woman would think of her.

Jean shook her head, "I didn't tell her."

There was something about the way she looked away that made Nicole wonder about the whole truth behind that statement. Before she could inquire T.J came running in.

"Mom, you look pretty." He threw his arms around her neck for a hug before stepping back. "Jason is waiting downstairs."

"Okay, Little Man, tell him I'll be right down." Nicole assured him and laughed as he raced back out of the room.

Chapter Seven

As they told everyone goodbye Nicole couldn't stop thinking about the conversation with her mother and knew that Rose would soon know everything. The two ladies had grown so close over the past few years that there were no secrets between them. She just hoped that Rose wouldn't think any less of her.

While they pulled out of the drive in Jason's car, she pushed those worries aside. They rode with the windows up and soft music paying in the radio.

She turned to him and smiled. "Are you going to tell me why we're leaving so early to go to dinner?"

He chuckled. "It was going to be a surprise but I see that you're too impatient for that. I thought I would show you around my neighborhood before we eat."

Glancing down at her shoes she remarked, "I may have chosen the wrong footwear."

He followed her glance but she didn't miss his eyes lingering on her bare legs. When his eyes met hers for a moment, she'd seen the signs of desire in them.

"We shouldn't be doing too much walking." he replied.

Crossing her legs and adjusting the hem of her sundress she smiled to herself when he glanced again. "Good."

"I noticed your mother came to see you."

"Yes." Nicole looked out of her window. "She knows the truth about us."

"How?"

"She wondered about out argument and the way things fell into place once we spent some time alone. I saw no reason to lie, she already knew that I met someone on the cruise."

"How do you feel about them knowing?" he asked, then at her questioning look he added, "I assume that Rose knows as well."

"It was bound to come out sooner or later." she replied with a shrug. She didn't want to start the date off badly so she didn't admit that she was worried. So, she changed the subject. "The weather turned out nice for the outing."

He nodded. "I've learned never to take fair weather for granted."

She listened to him talk about some of the bad weather he'd encountered in his work for F.E.MA. She was amaze at how much he had seen and done while she'd lived a mundane life in her small home town. Would she be enough to hold him if he got another offer? After all, he'd gotten to travel while doing what he loved and making good money.

"You're being quiet." he commented after a few minutes.

Shaking her head to clear her thoughts she explained, "I'm envious of the places you've seen. Even at their worst times they each seem to have captured a piece of your heart."

"Maybe I should consider writing poetry." he joked, causing her to giggle. "You never heard of the Physicists Poet?"

"I think my professors may have skipped over that one, is he very well known?"

"Just among other Physicists," came his quick reply, making her laugh again.

"You can travel now, you know." he said, serious. "Even if you wanted to go without T.J. he would be looked after."

"I'm not sure I would feel comfortable with that." she was honest. "Maybe I should start with the two of us going somewhere."

"Did you and David ever vacation together?"

She twirled a strand of hair that she's left loose, around her finger. "Just a short Honeymoon. After that he was busy with other things."

She disliked when he asked her questions about her marriage, but she felt she owed him her honesty. But was aware that he knew enough now to read between the lines to find what she wasn't saying. "But I've been meaning to take T.J. to Disney World before he out grows it. I've never been either so it'll be a first for both of us. Mostly, it's something just for fun, instead education."

"I've never been, but my two oldest are going over the holiday."

"You mentioned that. It's a shame that I won't get to meet them."

"You just want some embarrassing stories about me." he said "Seth will give you enough ammo when he visits."

"That's only fair. You've heard your share about me."

It wasn't long until they were crossing into the city lines of Atlanta. Jason navigated well as they headed I to areas Nicole wasn't familiar with. These tree lined streets could fit in with New Hope. Children were riding bikes and at the park playing basketball.

Jason parked by the curb in front of the high school. "I thought we could stretch our legs here."

He got out and walked around to open the door for her. Taking his offered hand, she stepped out and smoothed her dress. Keeping her hand in his Jason began to stroll the campus grounds.

"We lived in a house a few blocks from here, so we walked. Since my brothers were all athletes, they had girls standing in line." He told her, as they came upon the athletic fields. He pointed to a tree a sitting in the middle of the fields, "That's where I would sit and study while they practiced."

"You didn't have girls waiting in line?" she teased.

"Maybe a couple that didn't just want to be introduced to my brothers."

She grinned as she squatted down to remove her shoes. When she stood back up, holding her shoes in one hand, she grabbed his hand with the other and led him under the shade tree. Dropping her sandles she turned and put her hands on his shoulders.

Looking into his warm grey eyes she told him, "Fools, all of them."

Just as she'd hoped his head came down and she stretched to meet him, their lips meeting in a slow exchange. It was just heated enough for them to forget their surroundings.

Until they heard someone cough discreetly to get their attention. And a deep voice remark, "I never thought I would catch you making out on campus, Matthews."

Jason chuckled and released her to turn in his arms. "Sorry, Coach, do I have detention?"

The other man chuckled. "That may have been the one thing to drag your father down here to protest. He never questioned it with your brothers."

Jason laughed as well. "He knew what they were capable of. Coach, this is Nicole. She's from New Hope. I was just showing her the old neighborhood."

The coach shook Jason's hand. "I'll let you get back to your fun. Just remember there are minors on campus. Nice to meet you, Nicole."

She giggled. "My pleasure."

As he walked back over to the ball field they walked back to the car as she tried to control her racing heart. She didn't understand how a simple kiss from him could make her feel more yearning than she'd felt in her entire marriage.

When they arrived back at his car, and he reached to open her door she stopped him. His brow raised in silent query.

"Thank you, for sharing this with me."

Stepping close to her, he tucked a strand of hair behind her ear. "There isn't a part of me that I wouldn't share with you." Then he opened her door, "Besides, we're not done."

They rode around the neighborhood and he pointed out the house they had grown up in. She didn't ask why they didn't stop, as she put her shoes back on, but couldn't stopped herself from wondering. She would be meeting them soon enough, she reminded herself.

Then they pulled into a parking lot beside what looked like a local neighborhood dive bar.

The building was old but freshly painted with neon signs in the windows.

She waited until he was helping her out of the car that she asked him, "What are we doing here? I thought we were having dinner."

"We are." he assured her, his hand on her lower back. "This is the surprise I didn't tell you about. We're having drinks with my brothers."

She stopped in her tracks, suddenly overcome with nerves. "Tell me you're kidding."

He looked down on her in concern. "No. All four Matthews brothers." Turning to face her he rubbed her bare arms with his hands. "Are you okay?"

She smiled up at him, "Certainly, it's just unexpected."

"You were just saying it was ashamed you wouldn't get to meet all of them." he reminded her. "And I've already met your family."

"That's not the same thing. You didn't know who they were."

He chuckled. "I didn't arrange those circumstances. Are you alright with this?"

"It's just some butterflies. I'll be fine." she assured him.

Putting his arm around her, he led her inside. It was early enough that it wasn't too crowded, and it was easy to spot his brothers at a table by the wall. They were all tall, with the same strong build as Jason. Standing beside the table as they all rose, Nicole found herself the center of their gazes.

Blushing, she shook each of their hands as introduced, before taking the seat Jason held out for her. They all had the same straight nose and jaw. All brunette, with the exception of Seth, who was blond.

"So, this is her?" Chad broke the silence. "The one that got away."

"Excuse me?" she asked.

"Unlike your family, mine knows all the details of our relationship." Jason teased. "As the eldest Glen still thinks it's his job to keep us in our place."

"What did you tell them about me?"

"That I met a beautiful, intelligent woman and let her slip away." he took her hand in his under the table.

As soon as the server took their order and let Nicole turned to the two oldest brothers, "I hear that you two are taking your families to Disney world for the holiday."

It was Glen that answered, excitedly, "We've been saving for a while and we're finally doing it."

"I was just telling Jason earlier that I've never been. And I should take T.J. before he thinks he's too old." She looked at Chad with concern. "I hear your wife is almost due. Surely, she isn't going?"

"No, she'll be staying home. I hate to leave her but she insists." Chad confided.

"Why not bring her for the week as weel?" she asked Seth. "Not only will she not be alone, but she'll be pampered and spoiled."

When Chad hesitated, Jason told him. "It's true. She won't have to lift a finger all week."

"Please ask her." Nicole pleaded. "I've longed for someone else to get the treatment I did when I was expecting. The full royal treatment and she'll feel like a queen. It'll be like her own spa vacation."

Chad nodded. "I'll suggest it. She deserves it."

"Our younger brother says your son is almost as smart as he is." Glen remarked. "Was his father very smart?"

"He was smart enough to become an attorney, but not as smart as Jason or T.J." she answered feeling awkward again.

The server brought their drinks and they all began to tell stories of their childhood. She learned that boys were way worse on each other if they were related.

"Don't forget when he was seven and we put his hand in warm water after he was asleep to make him think he had a bed wetting problem." Chad told them. "Mom tore our asses up when she realized what we were doing."

"That wasn't funny." Jason spoke over his laughing brothers. "I was looking through medical books to find out what was wrong."

"We were just preparing you for what others were going to do when you started skipping grades." Chad told him.

"I only skipped two grades."

As she listened to the brothers, she once again wondered what she'd missed being an only child. She suddenly wanted more for T.J. Someone to keep him from becoming too serious minded, like Jason had. She hadn't considered it before but it made sense.

T.J. already worried about the problems of the world that he was too young to be so concerned with. He needed someone like Jason had with his brothers. Someone his age that could get him to be like a kid.

Jason squeezed her hand to get her attention, and she looked over at him he whispered, "Everything ok?"

She nodded. "Fine."

"Well, Nicole," Chad replied, "Maybe you will give us more details about the way you two met. Jason mentioned that you got him to go to the beach. He said that he would never swim in the ocean."

"He didn't swim, but I believe he enjoyed watching me go in the water." She had a sudden memory and smiled mischievously. "Until he got distracted by feeding the birds."

Jason met her gaze and frowned. "I told you that having a sea gull swoop down and take the sandwich I was holding is not feeding the birds."

"Let me ask you one question before I agree," she dared him.

His eyes narrowed on her, "What's the question?"

"Did the bird get fed?'

"Yes." he answered, hesitantly.

"Then, by logic, you fed the birds." She smiled, winningly.

Jason's mouth dropped open, then closed again, without speaking. His brothers hooted with laughter.

"Look at hm," Seth remarked. "He's speechless."

"It looks like little brother has met his match."

Ncole laughed. "Raising T.J. I've learned they can't argue with logic."

"There's a book that would sell." Jason commented. "How to raise a child genius."

She thought about it for a second, then changed the subject. "Did he tell you about the night I tried to teach him to dance?" she asked. "Your brother has no since of rhythm. He was so bad that he threw me off beat."

His brothers shared another laugh as she continued. Until Jason spoke up. "I thought you wanted to hear stories, not give them more ammunition against me."

Glen looked at two of them and said, "Maybe now that he's found you, he'll stay home for a change."

Sipping her drink, it took a moment for her to respond. "I'm not sure how much sway I have over that. "Some people feel the call of the open road and can't resist."

As Glen began to speak, Jason cut him off. "I'm not going anywhere any time soon."

Nicole looked between the brother, wondering what hadn't been said. Could it have been

about their mother? "I'm sorry. I didn't mean to bring up bad memories."

Not it was their time to be confused. Or at least Chadd and Glen were.

Seth chucked. "She thinks she reminded us of Mom."

"I know what it's like having a parent disappear from your life. I should have been more sensitive." she continued.

They all laughed then and Jason put his arm around her and squeezed. "We've all come to terms with it. Don't worry that you've upset anyone."

Chad checked his watch, "As much as I've enjoyed this, I need to get home to the family."

Glen stood as well, and they all hugged before the two oldest left. Then Seth told Nicole and Jason, "I know that you two have dinner plans, so go ahead."

"You're staying alone?" Nicole asked.

Jason grinned and replied, "I don't think he plans on being alone for long."

"Oh, right." Nicole felt herself blush again. "Good night then."

THINGS WERE GOING AS well as Jason had planned so far. Nicole had been nervous meeting his brothers, at first, but had loosened up to them soon enough. Sharing the stories about their meeting had made him realize the two of them never discuss those memories. He'd began to wonder how much she remembered from then.

They stopped at a popular burger joint that he and his brothers had frequented growing up. She looked gorgeous in her sundress that matched her eyes, with her hair pulled back with a few loose strands. As much as he enjoyed her family, especially T.J., it was nice to be alone with her.

He leaned across the table and spoke in a husky whisper, "That dress matches your eyes. It reminds me of the one you wore the night we first met."

She leaned forward as well. "I thought the same thing when I selected it."

He kissed the back of her hand. "You still look just as beautiful."

The way she blushed at every comment angered him, because she should be used to them. She'd had a fool for a husband and he wondered if she realized that.

"I believe my brothers like you." he told her. "They didn't know what to expect."

"I'm glad I didn't disappoint them." She took a drink.

"It made me realize that we don't talk about our time together on the cruise." he reached to cup her free hand in his, "and I wondered why?"

She tried to pill her hand away but he tightened his grip, slightly, until she ceased. "It's just that you got so angry when you learned the truth that I haven't wanted to remind you when things are going so well."

He raised a brow. "Do you think so?"

"Of course, why do you ask?"

He smiled, "I've been worrying about disappointing you."

"I don't think that's possible." she spoke, softly. "So far, you have been perfect."

"I'm glad you think so." he stood and pulled her chair out. "Time to head back to New Hope." He was pleased when she looked disappointed. "Don't worry, the night's not over yet."

On the ride back to New Hope they kept the conversation light. He kept his hand alternating between his fingers fingering the loose strands of her hair and laying on her naked knee. He felt every time she shivered in response and couldn't keep from smiling to himself.

Reaching the outskirts of the small town he turned in the opposite direction and it didn't escape her notice.

"You're going the wrong way?' she remarked.

He glanced over at her, "I told you the night wasn't over yet."

There was enough light now to see dawning on her face. She put her hand on his where it rested now on her thigh. "Are we going where I think we are?"

He nodded. "I have some champagne and strawberries waiting."

"How did you manage that?"

"I got the key from your mother," he admitted. This time he was blushing. "I didn't ask she came and slipped it to me a couple of days ago."

Nicole covered her eyes with her free hand. "Oh, no. What did she say?"

"Nothing. She came to the library when T.J. was getting some cookies, slid it across the desk to me and walked out."

She suddenly giggled. "She's not even bothering to hide it anymore."

"They are losing their subtlety." he admitted.

He pulled into the yard that was lit by the porch light he'd left on, as well a couple of lamps inside. He turned to her and found her looking at him in wonder. He smiled and got out of the car.

After helping her out, and closing the door, he took her in his arms for a kiss. His plans for the rest of the night kept him from pressing her against the side of his car, and kept his desire under control.

When the kiss this ended, he took her hand in his and led her up the steps and inside. He watched in silence as she looked around at the roses sitting around the room. The soft light from the lamps lit the highlights in her hair, and made her skin glow.

He kissed her cheek. "You sit on the sofa while I bring everything from the kitchen."

He took the champagne and strawberries from the fridge, and set them on a tray before getting the two glasses. He worked quickly and headed back to the living room.

He set the tray on the table before sitting beside her. He was surprised and alarmed when he saw tears in her eyes. His hands went to her shoulders to turn her toward him. "What's wrong?"

Shaking her head, she spoke softly. "Nothing."

"Then why the tears?"

"I just can't believe you arranged all of this." she confessed. "No one has ever made me feel so special."

He pressed her against him and wrapped her in his in a hug. "That's a shame because I can't think of anyone who deserves it more."

After a moment she pulled out of his arms, and laughed nervously. "I'm sorry. I'm ruining your surprise."

He wiped her remaining teas with his thumbs. "It's not ruined."

Once she smiled, he turned to pour them each a drink. Giving her a glass, he offered her a strawberry from a plate. She took one and bit into it, licking the juice from her lips, and he had to adjust his seat. She held the other half up for him and he ate it with pleasure.

It was quiet as they fed each other strawberries, and drank a couple glasses. When he felt he couldn't stand it anymore, he took her glass and set theirs both back down. She went into his arms immediately.

The air smelled of roses, and she tasted of strawberries and her own sweetness. With one arm around her waist and the other holding at the back of her neck, he pulled her across his lap. Then he drowned in the warmth and softness of her. As their mouths melded together, he let his hands run over her curves, from breast to her knee.

He felt her gasp as one hand cover her breast. She repositioned herself to straddle his thighs, giving him greater access to the places he wished to reach. His lips traveled to her ear and down her neck to her shoulder as he pulled the straps down until her luscious mounds were uncovered, expect for the white lace bra she wore.

He felt her head fall back as his lips pressed between them, with lace still covering them he teased one nipple, knowing the lace would add to the pleasure she felt. He let his hand travel up one thigh, beneath her dress to feel a bare cheek of her buttock.

He leaned back to see her smiling wickedly down at him, "You're not the only one with surprises up their sleeve."

Feeling further he felt the strap in back that led to more lace covering her sweet spot. "Are they white too?"

She nodded before leaning down and covering his mouth with hers, and rubbed her breasts against his shirt. But if she had any illusions about hurrying this along, she was in for a surprise.

Holding her steady by the waist he let his fingers wonder between her spread legs. At first, he kept his touch light, just barely brushing over the lace. When she tried to move against his fingers his other arm circled her waist to press her body to his, holding her immobile.

She moaned her frustration against his lips, and he gave in, giving her more. Using the texture of the lace on her here, as well. Pulling on the strap he rubbed the lace against her, driving her to gasp for breath. Taking advantage, her lifted a little higher and teased her nipples again.

By the time his fingers moved between her thighs again the thong was damp from her growing passion. Sliding a finger inside, he felt her body try to pull it in further, but he pulled out again, to thrust it back in. Even as he brought her closer to the edge, he could feel himself grow harder beneath his jeans.

She was riding his fingers now, looking for release, and he let her have it. She was panting
in his ear and he told her, "It's time to move to the bed."

"I'm not sure that I can walk there."

He slid the straps over her dress back up, so that her arms could hold on around his neck. "I'll be more than happy to carry you."

He stood with her in his arms, and her legs circled his waist, causing her to brush against the hardness in the front of his jeans. Once in her room, lit by a lamp as well. She slid sensually down his body. He sat her on her feet, made sure she was steady, before slid the straps of her dress down and letting it fall to the floor.

He stood back to remove his own clothes, watching her stand there with her eyes half closed in her matching lace bra and thong, still in her heels. When she licked her lips, he hoped it was because she found him as pleasing to the eyes as he did her.

Once he was naked, he let her eyes rake him over once before taking her in his arms once again. He was taking his time tonight, doing all of the things to her that he'd been dreaming about all of these years.

Stepping directly in front of her he reached up to undo the front clasp of her bra. He saw her breath hitch in her throat and smiled tenderly. "As lovely as this is, I think that we could do without it now."

She nodded and shivered as he let in fall in the way of her dress. Giving her a light kiss before kneeling in front of her, he reached for the straps at her hips, lowering the thong for her to step out of. He softly ran his hands back up to her waist. He kissed the tender skin above her curls, and inhaled her musky scent.

She let out a whimper as he done no more than lift her to sit on the side of the bed, her legs still hanging of the side. He lifted one foot and took of her high heel, massaging her foot as he kissed her ankle, up to her knee, before laying that leg over his shoulder.

He repeated the process with the other, until both legs were over his shoulders, and she had laid back. He kissed both thighs before letting his tongue run through her damp curls until he found the little nub, already swollen, and began to flick it lightly. When her hips began to move in response, he took her by the waist to hold her still as he drove her toward that peak again. Stopping just before she could fall over it without him.

Kissing his way up her body, he managed to reposition them vertical on the bed. He entered her bit by bit, loving the feel of her heat pulling him deeper. He made love to her slowly, using his hands and mouth to caress the rest of her, until she was writhing beneath them. Taking his time, he reveled in her every moan and caress. Feeling her release coming he let himself go and they flew over into bliss together.

After catching his breath, he slid to her side and pulled her against his chest. He'd had a startling thought that he was trying to come to grips with. It wasn't that he couldn't fall in love, because he had years ago. It was that he couldn't love anyone else. He held her tight, not wanting her to disappear on him again.

Chapter Eight

Nicole felt as if she were floating, except for Jason arms tight around her, and her every muscle languid. Although his embrace was almost too tight, she felt warm, safe, and cared for. It was a new feeling to lay with a man and feel those things.

She was beginning to have strong feelings for him and wondered if he was feeling the same. She wanted to spend the night, and wake up in his arms, but knew that wasn't possible. She sighed heavily against his chest.

"Is something wrong?" He drew her face up to look at him.

"I was thinking that it's a shame that we have to leave." She laid her head back on his chest. "It's not the same at home."

She felt his body stiffen and looked up to find him frowning at her.

"I've noticed that I just don't understand why."

She sat up, and looked at him over her shoulder, "What do you mean? It would just be uncomfortable for everyone."

He moved stiffly to sit on the side of the bed with his back to her as he grabbed his jeans to put on. "No one is uncomfortable but you."

Leaning over the side of the bed, she fished up her dress and throw it on over her head.

"Why do you say that?"

"Everyone in that house knows what's going on, even planned it, do you really believe that they wouldn't want to see the results of their plotting?"

"Jason, you don't understand. That's David's home, where he grew up. I'm only allowed to stay there now because Rose wants to be close to her grandson."

He turned in her then, glaring at her through dark eyes. "T.J. isn't the only reason she keeps you around. And don't try to tell me it's out of respect for her. If you're trying to respect anyone, it's the memory of your husband. And for the life of me I can't understand why you would want to show him respect now, when he never showed you any when he was alive."

She jerked as if he's slapped her. How could he make her feel so safe, then say something to hurt her that way, "Get out."

Jerking his shirt on he told her, "If that's how you want it." Then he walked out.

She sat on the side of the bed, stunned. How could a night that had been going so well went so wrong?

Shaking her head, she pulled her phone from her purse. First thing she needed was a ride home. She hit speed dial and Summer answered immediately.

After she quickly explained, and Summer was on her way, she rose and finished dressing. When she made her way to the front door, she noticed some parking lights. Surely Summer hadn't arrived that quickly.

Peeking out of a window she was surprised to see Jason's car still there. He couldn't possibly think that she was getting in the same car with him. At present, she wasn't sure if she was angrier or upset. Either way she didn't trust herself in such a confined space as his car.

She stayed inside until she saw Summer's headlights pull in. She walked straight to the passenger side of her friend's car and got in.

"I thought he had left." Summer remarked. "Why is he still here?"

"I don't care." she answered, coldly.

Summer didn't comment as she backed out and started driving them across town. She noticed Jason behind them but gave no indication, just sat in silence, looking out her window.

"Would you like to talk about it?" Summer asked her.

"I don't know." She held her hands out to indicate she was at a loss as to what went wrong. "We were having a good time, and he brought me back here for drinks...."

"I'm sure the two of you had more than drinks." Summer teased.

"Of course." Nicole managed a small smile at the teasing remark. "We were laying in the afterglow when I made a remark about hating to have to leave because it wasn't the same when we're with the family. Suddenly he was angry at me. How can someone go from making you feel so safe, even cherished, to making me want to hit him over the head with something heavy."

"What did he say to make you feel that way?"

"He said that he couldn't understand why I'm trying to give David such much respect in death when he never gave me any in life." she paused at her friend's gasp. "I told him to get out."

They rode in silence a few moments when Nicole spoke up again, "You have nothing to say?"

"Not when you're already angry at him."

Nicole turned to the other woman and accused, "You agree with him."

"Oh, look, we're here." Summer parked in the circular drive, before looking at Nicole. "Come over tomorrow and we can talk about it after you've had time to think and cool down."

"Coward." Nicole opened her door and got out.

"True. I've seen you angry." Summer replied, playfully. Then turned serious, "Even if I agree with him, Jason was much harsher than he should have been."

"Thank you." Nicole told her as she shut the door.

Heading to the door she didn't acknowledge him when he got out of his own car and followed her inside. The nerve of him telling her how to behave. Any woman in her position would feel the same way in her circumstances.

It wasn't until they were standing in front of their respective doors that he started to speak,

"Nic...,"

She opened her door, walked in, and shut it on his words. She couldn't listen to any more tonight about how she wasn't what he expected her to be. She knew that she wasn't living up to his expectations, but she wasn't the same person as she was when they first met. She had other people to consider now, not just herself.

Leaning against the door, she let the tears she'd been holding start to flow.

THE COUPLE THOUGHT everyone had gone to bed, but Rose and Jean were talking in the study. They heard the door open and close, and then a silence that spoke volumes. Any couple coming in after a good night out would be whispering and giggling.

Rose looked over to her friend. "I thought you said they had worked things out."

"That's what she told me." Jean replied. "They must have fought over something else. Now, tell me what is going on in that head if yours."

Rose shook her head. "No, I'm not certain yet."

"Certain about what." Jean pressed. "I went and talked to her, told you things I'm sure she

would rather you didn't know, tell me what's going on."

"I'm afraid that I'm about to lose my family." Rose's voice was barely above a whisper. She told her friend her worries, what she suspected, and what she was most afraid of. "Rose, she would never do that. She's not just here because of T.J., she's here because she loves you. We all do."

Rose smiled at her friend. "Enough about me. What's concerning you?"

"I'm concerned that my marriage had effects on her that I hadn't realized before." Jean admitted. "Maybe it's my fault that she doesn't know what a healthy relationship is. I put up with her father for much longer than I should have."

"You're afraid that's why she stayed with my son when most would have at least left him. Most would have left, with the child, and made sure that he had no money to support his whore."

"I would never speak ill of the dead."

"That's why I done it for you." Rose shook her head sadly. "We knew what he was, but we couldn't change him. I think he still had hopes that we would accept that woman, right up until he died."

"Do you ever wonder if you made the right choice? Maybe he did love Clair." Jean replied.

"As much as I hate how their marriage went, and how much she suffered, I'm glad to have had Nicole for a daughter-n-law. And you as a sister. Some things I would change, some I wouldn't."

"The real question is what so we do now?"

"Let me sleep on it. Maybe something will come to me."

DESPITE THE LONG, HOT bath she had taken, Nicole had gotten very, little sleep, and couldn't face a breakfast with so much tension between the two of them. She stood in front of her mirror now, studying her red, swollen eyes and preparing a cold cloth.

Laying down and putting it over her eyes, she tried to think out the problem. No matter what she done she felt as if someone were being hurt. Then she thought, again, about what Jason had said.

She couldn't believe a man that had given her the greatest pleasure she'd ever known could, only moments later, give her the greatest pain she'd ever felt. It still stung that he would say such a thing when he knew what he did. All she was trying to do was be a decent person.

An hour later she was dressed in shorts and top, her hair pulled back. When she arrived downstairs, she found Charles, with his children, gathered in the hallway. Rose looked overjoyed as she hugged each one, before leading them through the house and out to the garden.

Charles stopped and gave Nicoel a hug. "We cleared out. Get as loud as you like."

She nodded and grabbed her purse. It was a quick drive through town, but Nicoel enjoyed the wind coming through her windows.

She found her friend in the kitchen, cleaning up the breakfast dishes. She walked over to the coffee make and proceeded to make herself a cup.

They both sat at the table and Nicole took a sip of coffee. "Charles thought that we were going to argue."

Summer shrugged and sat her cup down. "That depends on what I learn and if you're reasonable."

"Since I'm usually a reasonable person, what do you need to learn?" she replied with a smile.

"Well, you and Jason seem to do fine when you're away from the house." Summer began, "How do you two behave then?"

"What do you mean?"

"Do you hold hands? Steal kisses in the hallway?" Summer clarified. "Any P.D.A.s at all?"

"We walk through the garden in the evenings. We share everything there." Nicole put it simply.

"Has he tried to hold your hand around others?"

Not able to meet her friend's gaze Nicole lifted her cup again. "A couple of times."

Summer sounded exasperated. "Tell me you didn't pull away."

"It's uncomfortable. David grew up in that house and it doesn't seem right." She stressed. "I thought as a woman that you would understand."

"If you had a marriage like mine, I would agree with you." Summer assured her. "But I think Jason is right in your case.

David made your life miserable when he was alive. Why would you let him continue to do so in death? You deserve to be happy." When Nicole didn't instantly agree she speculated, "Unless this is another excuse."

"Now, what are on about?"

"You're using that house to keep distance between you." Summer's head tilted in thought. "Yes, that makes more sense. You have always run from being hurt. That's why you chose David in the first place- Not because you couldn't hurt him, but because he could never hurt you."

"That's ridiculous." Nicole protested. She stood and walked over to look out to the window by the back door. "Besides, it seems he did manage to hurt me."

Concern coloring her voice, Summer asked, "What do you mean?"

She turned to face her friend. "Not emotionally, but the way I see myself." She sat back down. "His preference for Clair has made me feel like I'm not enough to keep any man's affection."

Summer reached across the table to squeeze her hands that were clasped in front of her. "You never hinted at anything."

"I've just recently realized it myself. I guess it took me wanting to keep someone around." She laughed softly. "Maybe you're right and I'm trying to keep a wall between us."

"What are the most afraid of?"

Starring into her coffee she asked, "What if I fall in love and he gets a call that they need him in some disaster area and he goes?"

"First, I don't think that man is going anywhere. Second, that's no longer his job."

"Why do you think he's not going anywhere? His brothers talk as if it were just a matter of time."

"Honey, as angry as he must have been last night, he didn't leave. He stayed to make sure you would get home safely. I believe that his brothers may have been teasing him." Summer told her. "Guys do that, especially if they're related. And you don't see the say he looks at you. You didn't see the look on his face when I told him that you had been trying to find him. I think he's in the same place you are."

"How do I know for sure?" she wondered aloud. "About him or me?"

Summer laughed. "If you're not in love, then you're halfway there. You aren't going to believe gestures. I think the two of you should have a serious talk." her friend added. "This is between the two of you. The people that love you just want you to be happy."

They went into the living room and watched a movie, but Nicole's mind was on other

things.

She thought herself in circles until Charles came back with the kids. Turns out they had been called over to cheer Rose up. Worrying about what had the older lady down she quickly gave them goodbye hug and headed out.

On the drive home she thought about everything they had discussed and decided they were right. There was no denying that she felt differently for Jason than any man before. She wanted to be with him all of the time and when she wasn't her thoughts were consumed by him. The most telling was the deep jealousy she had felt seeing him with Clair.

Was her best friend right. Was she halfway there? If she was, was she brave enough to reach for it. To take a chance on her and loose her heart. Maybe they should have a long talk. But would he be willing.

She supposed that she would find out tonight. If he hadn't approached her by dinner time, she would take things into her own hands. Even if she had to corner in his room. Grinning to herself, she thought that had promise.

Chapter Nine

Jason hadn't been surprised when Nicole had taken off, he couldn't blame her. He *had* been surprised to see Charles and happy to be distracted by meeting his children. The young girl seemed out-numbered but she could more than hold her own against the boys she was growing up with.

They supervised the children in the garden, while Rose watched them play tag. They talked about several things until Jason finally brought it up.

"So, are you going to ask."

"Nah, I figured if you wanted to talk, you would," Charles told him. "I also thought you would rather speak with one of your brothers."

"Do you realize how much damage that man done to her? He broke her."

Charles nodded. "We just needed her to wake up and see it. I believe she's starting to."

That was all they said about Nicole but Jason hadn't stopped thinking about her. He was ashamed of the way he acted. But having reality hit him just after the revelation he'd had, made him feel jealousy at being reminded of who's house they were living in. He'd spoken in anger, and hurt her, the one thing he never wanted to do.

He'd left soon after she arrived back home, going into town to eat. He wanted to speak with her, to apologize., but not in front of the family. She had needed to hear what he'd said, but not tossed out in a fit of anger.

He was in love with her, had been from their first meeting, and he wanted to shout it to the world, but not as long as he wasn't sure where her heart truly lay. Fingering the velvet bag, he'd been holding he heard her door open across the hall. He would give her a few minutes before following her.

The knock on his door startled him so much that he called for then to enter before he thought about what he was wearing. He'd moved to get off of the bed, seeing it was Nicole he leaned back against the headboard again.

She wore the robe silk robe he was familiar with, and had brushed her hair out so that it hung to her shoulders. Her hands were clasped together and her feet were bare.

"I thought that we could talk." she spoke, hesitantly.

He took the fact that she was in his room as a good sign. Indicating the side of the bed he said, "Please, have a seat."

She appeared to steel her spine, but walked over an sat on the bed. He sat with his legs stretched out, in only a pair boxer shorts, and he didn't miss the way her eyes ran over him. Folding his arms across his chest to keep from reaching out for her, he waited for her to start.

"I wanted to apologize for not considering your feelings about the way I behave here. I convinced myself that you understood, when I was the one being irrational."

He held up a hand to stop her speech. "You were being respectful, and if it was any other situation, I would agree with you. And I'm sorry I shouted out something that should have been discussed calmly."

"You have every right to your feelings, and to expect me to consider them in this relationship." She crawled onto the bed to kneel by his thighs. "David and I weren't the kind of couple for P.D.A, maybe if we had really loved one another, it would have been different."

"Do you want us to be a couple, a real couple?"

She gave him a sweet smile and admitted to him. "The problem is I'm scared of my feelings for you and that was a way of keeping some distance between us. I don't want to do that anymore." Her hands came up to caress his chest.

Reaching out and taking her hands in his, "First, tell me, have you shared either of these rooms with him."

She shook her head. "When we shared a room, it was the one Rose is in. I insisted she take the master bedroom back. That was the only place."

"Good," he said, before pulling her up and over until she fell across his chest

Her response was to laugh, playfully, and adjust to sit straddling his thighs. She set her hands on his shoulders, but when she leaned in to kiss him, he stopped her.

Seeing the hurt and confused expression he explained, "We don't have to rush. Just let me look at you."

He studied her face, clear of any make up, from her blue eyes down to her rounded chin. Then he used his fingers to trace the lines of her face, lingering on her pink lips. His hands dropped to her shoulder to slid the robe off. She untied it at the waist. Before dropping her arms so that it fell to her wrists.

Taking it and tossing it toward the chair, and looked at what she wore beneath. Made of white silk it clung to her curves and he could see her the shadow her nipples through it. He took a moment to be thankful how lucky he was before, leaning her forward for a slow kiss.

Tonight, he didn't want passion, but to wallow in their newly revealed feelings they had for one another. Keeping the kiss soft, and his hands holding her face, he managed to keep their bodies at a distance.

When her hands, that had been laying on his shoulders slid down to caress his chest, he pulled her forward and trapped them between them. She seemed determined to prover herself to someone, either herself or him, and it wasn't necessary. When she moved her hips to rub against his erection, he groaned and pushed her away, catching her hands in his.

"You don't have to do this." he told her.

"But I want to."

"But is it for the right reasons?" he inquired. "For now, it's enough for me to see that you're trying. I've just learned that you have real feelings for me, and I just want to hold you and be happy in that knowledge."

He saw tears glistening in her eyes and know they were happy ones. "And I just want you to hold me all night."

"Will anyone be looking for you across the hall?"

"If they do, I'm sure they'll figure it out."

He nodded and bent to pull the sheet up over them. They lay in each other's arms, sharing quick kisses, and light touches before she drifted off to sleep.

He wasn't sure how long he laid awake marveling that she was in his arms for the night, but afraid that when he slept that she would be gone in the morning.

OVER THE NEXT WEEK it seemed as if they couldn't pass one another without touching. They whispered and laughed through dinner, and more than once had been come upon while embracing. Everyone seemed to find it amusing, except T.J., who would wrinkle his nose and leave.

They slept in each other's arms every night, not always making love, sometimes just cuddling and talking about the day. She didn't have to ask Summer if she was falling in love, she knew that she was, more so with each passing day.

She still sometimes worried that she wouldn't be enough to hold him here, but shoved the thought away quickly, deciding not to borrow trouble. Her only real worry was Rose. Her mother-in-law seemed quiet and withdrawn, and she intended to leave early to talk to the older woman.

But day dreams kept her from concentrating on inventory as lunch slipped by. She was about to give up when her friend stuck her head in the door.

"Why have you been shut in here all morning?" Summer came and took her seat in front of the desk.

"I've been trying to get through this inventory and decide what to order, but I keep getting distracted." She explained.

Summer nodded. "Daydreaming, yeah you have all of the symptoms."

Nicole shared a smile with her, before turning serious. "I wanted to get home early and talk to Rose. She's been down this week."

"And you want to know what's causing it." Summer guessed. "Other than that, is everything going alright?"

"Couldn't be better." Nicole told her, finding it hard to describe, how happy she was. "Since I've dropped my wall at the house, we've gotten along great. We're getting ready for the holiday, and arrival of his father and younger brother. It's the only thing that makes Rose excited these days. Except when T.J. ask if we could get a pet."

"Wow. What kind of pet does he want? Are you making a trip to the pet store in the city?"

Nicole shook her head. "He's requested to get a dog from the shelter. Instead paying for an expensive one that we could donate the money to the shelter."

Summer's eyes widened for a moment, then she giggled. "Most kids his age wouldn't come up with that. Makes it hard to say no."

She grinned at the memory. "Rose was so happy with his suggestion she couldn't ither. Though I'm not sure her were caused by pride or sadness."

"I'm sure you're worried about nothing." Summer moved to another subject. "Are you nervous to meet his family?"

"I've already met Seth." She reminded the other woman. "But his father is a different story. And I do hope I can be friends with his sister-in-law."

"Don't worry. They're bound to like you." Summer stood. "I have an idea. Why don't you let the manager you hired take care of this and you go on home?"

"I don't know." She had insisted on hiring a manager in case she couldn't be there, but she'd yet to leave the younger girl on her own.

Summer went to the door, "Stacy, could you come in here please." Then she went around the desk and pulled Nicole out of her chair. "Go home and don't come back until I call you. You haven't taken a vacation since we opened, so I'm going to make you."

"Summer," she started to protest.

"We're not hearing it." Summer said, as Stacy arrived. "Stacy, the boss is taking a week off to spend with her handsome new man, are you ready?"

Stacy grinned. "Of course, I am." Then to Nicole, "We're all so happy for you. Go and enjoy yourself."

Blushing, she grabbed her purse and turned to leave. "Thanks."

After pulling from her spot, and getting over her embarrassment, she couldn't help but laugh. It seemed as if everyone was glad to see her move on with her life. She was afraid that people would disapprove of her having a male friend n David's home, but no one seemed to view it the way she had.

She and Jason didn't make love every night but they did share the same bed. They would lay in each other's arms and talk about their day, sharing secrets that no one else knew. Sometimes they would make out like teenagers, seeing who could last the longest before giving in to their desire.

She entered the house and walked up to her bedroom to freshen up with a new top before looking for Rose. She had just slipped the new shirt over her head when she heard the door open, and softly close.

She smiled when muscular arms encircled her waist. Jason nuzzled her ear a s he asks, "Why home so early?"

"I was so distracted that I was sent home for a week to enjoy the new man in my life." she stated, then added, teasingly, "Have you seen him around?"

He kissed the side of her neck. "I told him that you were already claimed."

She turned in his arms and ran her hands up his chest to his shoulders. "Is that right?"

His grin was wicked, "I thought that I had claimed you pretty completely. Do I need to remind you?"

She raised her brow at him in challenge, which he instantly took her up on. When their lips met, she melted against him instantly. She let herself enjoy the warmth of his embrace for a few minutes before stepping back.

"I'm sorry but I need to go talk to Rose." she explained. "I need to find out what's wrong."

He nodded in understanding. "She's in her solar."

"Thanks for understanding."

They held hands until they parted at the top of the staircase- where he went back down and she continued unto the next hallway. She found Rose in the small room at the end. There were several chairs and a sofa, with books scattered around.

Rose came here when she wanted to think, and she and Jean spent many nights here talking. But Nicole had only been in here a hand full of times. Rose was sitting in one of a matching pair of antique arm chairs, knitting. and raised her head when she heard Nicole enter.

"I was wondering if we could talk." she said from the doorway.

"Of course, my dear," Rose replied. "Come in and have a seat."

Nicole approached to sit in the matching armchair. There was a table between them with a lamp lit.

"I know that I've been preoccupied lately," she started, nervously. "But I have noticed that you seem a bit down lately, and wondered if there was anything that I can do."

"It's nothing for you to worry about, it's a part of growing old."

"So, it's not having Jason and I behaving as a couple here." She spoke, cautiously. "Or something my mother may have told you last week."

Rose put her knitting away and looked at Nicole through the dim light of the lamp. "Yes, your mother told me about your knowing Jason before you were married, and if my son had treated you decently, I would be furious. But as it was, I was lucky when you decided to marry him anyway. As for you and Jason, I wanted this for you, and the only sorrow it brings me is to make me miss my Thomas." Rose took her hands that lay on her lap. "There's nothing you could do to make me disappointed in you."

Nicole just nodded, "And I want you to know that no matter what happens between myself and Jason, I would never keep T.J. away from you. He will always love you because you're his grandmother that dotes on him."

"Thank you for saying that." Rose picked her knitting back up. "I don't know what I would do if I lost him as well."

OVER THE NEXT COUPLE of days, they made sure to include Rose in their plans as much as she would allow. She agreed to go to the animal shelter, as long as they stopped for supplies on the way.

While Rose spoke to an employee about getting supplies; she Jason, and T.J. picked out a collar, leash, as well as food and water dishes. Nicole was watching the two of them pick out some toys when she felt someone watching her, but glancing around she found no one.

Shrugging the feeling off she went to join Rose in the front of the store. "I'm glad you joined." she told her mother-in-law.

Rose's arm circled her waist. "I'm enjoying myself. I was just telling the manager about my grandson's suggestion. I'm so proud."

"We all are." She agreed, then confided, "I've been thinking about taking on a writing project."

Rose smiled widely as she turned to Nicole. "That's terrific. What kind?"

She told her mother-in-law about Jason's suggestion while having drinks with his brothers. "I've been thinking about it, and I believe it could work. I sure have the first-hand experience for it."

"I think that it's perfect." Rose told her. "I remember when you talked about writing all of the time. I'm glad to hear you didn't give it up."

They continued discussing the project until Jason and T.J. joined them. They quickly paid for their purchases and headed to the animal shelter.

T.J. seemed intent on giving each animal some attention while he decided which one to take home. Jason stayed with him while the ladies watched and spoke with the woman that ran the shelter.

"Your young men are unloading what we brought." Rose was telling her. "There will also be a delivery later today. As well as this donation." She handed the young brunette a check.

"Ms. Taylor, thank you so much." Tonya said.

"Thank my grandson." Rose told her proudly. "He said he wanted to rescue one and make a donation here instead of buying from a pet store."

"It's still very generous of all of you." Tonya replied.

It was then that T.J. called from the back. "Mom, Grandma, come here."

Nicole giggled. "I wonder what he's found."

Rose hooked her arm through Nicole's. "Let's go find out."

All three searched until they found Jason and her son looking into a cage with a pair of dogs. One was clearly a miniature poodle of some kind and the other seemed to be her baby, but with hair wasn't as curly.

"Why is there a mother and puppy here?" Rose asked.

Tonya looked at the pair sadly as she explained, "She was dropped of a couple of months ago with six puppies. Her owner was disappointed to see that she'd mated with a Jack Russel of some sort. Since she would never have pure bred puppies, he dropped them off here. That's here last puppy."

Rose leaned down and asked T.J., who nodded. She straightened back up and told Tonya. "We'll take them both."

Tonya actually threw her arms around the older woman. "Oh, thank you." she stepped back. I've been dreading her losing the last one. I'll go get the papers ready."

Jason helped by opening the cage and letting the dogs free. The poodle went straight to Rose and put her paws on her legs. Nicole leaned over to pick up the dog to carry only to have Rose hold her arms out.

"She'll be my new companion." Rose informed them and carried the dog toward the front.

Nicole and Jason shared a glance. But T.J. just grinned, picked up his puppy, and followed his grandmother.

OVER THE NEXT FEW DAYS Nicole got the same feeling she had while getting pet supplies, as if someone were watching her. Though she would look around she never found anything out of the ordinary.

Meanwhile they were getting ready for their guests the next day, and Rose sent them to the diner to pick up an order of pies.

T.J. was excited to have his coach arriving the next day, and couldn't stop talking about it. As Jason and he kept talking she spoke with the waitress about their order. She noticed a couple of customers whispering but she no longer cared what anyone said. When an elderly lady smiled at her she knew she was right in doing so.

Jason was carrying most of the tray, while T.J. helped, carrying the bags. They were on a few feet outside the door when she heard it reopen behind them.

Following her boys, Nicole wasn't going to turn until she heard a snide voice. "You should be a shame of yourself."

Freezing in her tracks, Nicole knew who it was before she turned around. "Jason, why don't the two of you go on to the car while I handle this."

He nodded, but she didn't miss the frown, and could guess what he was thinking. Only after they had started away did she turn to face the other woman.

"Why should I be?" she asked, coldly. "It's not like he's married."

Clair actually sneered at her. "How dare you judge me when you're the one that got pregnant by someone else and passed the baby off as David's. We always suspected, but never had any prove."

"What are you talking about?"

"David couldn't have been that boy's father. He couldn't have children."

Nicole almost laughed at the absurdity of that statement. Instead, she said, "I don't know what you're talking about."

"And now you have the nerve to bring your lover into the home of the man you trapped into marriage."

"I didn't trap David. I told him about the pregnancy and told him that I expected nothing from him." Nicole tried to remain calm. "He was the one that insisted on moving up the wedding, or did you forget that we were engaged."

"I remember. I also remember that he was pulling away from you and spending more time with me."

"I offered him an out and he didn't take it. I never planned to get pregnant." Nicole put ice in her voice. "He never denied being the father, which he could have, nor demanded a paternity test."

"Of course not." Clair's voice was like steel. "His father wouldn't have allowed anything different. The fact remains that you managed to get pregnant when he used protection with you and he never did with me. Yet we never conceived, although we were trying for years."

"If David isn't T.J.'s father, that is his name, not that boy." Nicole felt her anger rising. "Then who is?"

"The very man that you have taken as a lover again, and moved into the house of the man you claimed to love." Clair tossed out. "How could you disrespect him in such away?"

"I didn't bring anyone into the house." Nicole responded, barely containing her rage. "The tutor was Rose's idea. She put the word out, went through resumes, and dozens of interviews. Rose chose Jason for the position."

"Do you think people haven't noticed the resemblance between your lover and your son?" Clair snorted. "How did you think that you would get away with it? Do you think people are blind? They even have the same mannerisms. I don't know how you pulled the wool over that poor woman's eyes, but I mean to see she opens them."

She felt as if she'd been doused with cold water. Could it be true? Could she have made such a big mistake? But she refused to let the other woman see her doubts and shook the questions away. "You're either insane or missed your calling as a writer."

She turned and headed to the car with her back straight and head held high. But inside she was quivering with a realization that she may have made a gross miscalculation.

Smiling as she got into the car, her eyes met Jason's and she felt as if a hard lump had settled in her throat. After clearing it she said, "Sorry, just a little girl talk. Let's head home."

T.J. laughed from the backseat as Jason saluted her and pulled away from the curb. Jason held her hand on the console as they rode to the house.

The rest of the afternoon she watched Jason and T.J. together, and noticed that some of their gestures were the same. It could be that the young boy was mimicking his tutor, but he'd always done those gestures, she recognized them as natural.

The more closely she watched the more she was convinced that Clair had been right. Why hadn't she seen it? She'd been so sure since they had only the one night together, whereas she'd been with David numerous times with less protection.

She excused herself early for bed and took out some old photos. She laid a picture of her son next to a picture of her late husband at the same age on her desk and looked them over. With her eyes open to the possibilities, she could see the differences in them. It was more than just different coloring, the things she had attributed to her father or some long dead relation, all came from Jason. Even his intelligence.

How could she have been so blind?

Chapter Ten

There was a light tap on the door, before it slowly opened. Nicole quickly slipped the pictures under a stack of mail, and turned to see Jason closing the door.

"Are you positive that Clair didn't say anything to upset you?" he asked, tenderly.

She nodded.

"If you don't feel like my company tonight, I would understand."

"Don't even think about it." She got up, walked over to him, and put her arms around his waist. "I'm not going to let that woman ruin another moment of my life."

He tipped her chin up and gave her a tender kiss. "I'll give you a few moments and meet you in the garden."

"Okay." she stood on her toes and kissed his cheek. "I'll be down soon."

She watched him leave the room and felt as if there time together were drawing to a close. There was no doubt in her mind that he would be angry when she found the courage to tell him. And Rose would be heartbroken.

She didn't know what to do, and his family would be arriving tomorrow. She shouldn't approach the subject until after the holiday, there was no reason to spoil any of the plans.

Taking a deep breath, she began to change into her night cloths and robe. She opened her door to find her son about to knock.

"What is it, little man?"

"I was wondering something and Jason told me I should ask you." he explained. "Who was that lady earlier?"

Reaching for calm, she knelt down to his eye level. "She was a friend of David's." She couldn't stand to call him T.J.'s father now.

"She was his girlfriend?" he asked

She almost fell over at the question, and it took her a moment to find her voice. "How did you know about that?"

He shrugged. "I've heard things. Was it her?"

She gave hm a shaky smile because she couldn't find it in her to lie to him. "Yes, it was."

She was going to have to find a way to explain to him as well, she realized. They were all happy now, she should have known something was going to come along and mess it up. How was she going to explain her stupidity?

She walked her son to his room and tucked him in. Turning off the light and shutting the door, she made her way down through the kitchen to the garden.

There was a breeze blowing and a hint of rain in the air. The moon was peeking from between the clouds and seemed to spotlight where Jason waited for her. His hair was as dark as the night and his tanned arms opened in welcome.

Stepping into his embrace she let herself find comfort in the feel of his arms around her and the scent of cloves from his aftershave. Stepping back, but fingers intwined, they began their stroll through the rose bushes.

"You can be honest with me." Jason began. "What did Clair say?"

Nicole sighed before answering. "She blames me for the hard times that she's fallen in. She has it her head that I got pregnant to trap David into marriage."

"Why would she think that?"

"She claims that I felt David slipping away from me and didn't want to lose him." She could find some amusement from that accusation. "I was pulling away from him."

They came to the swing and sat, his arm around her shoulders. "Why was that?"

She shrugged. "I came back from that cruise with a new look on my life. I realized that I was settling for a life I never envisioned for myself. I got caught up in small town expectations instead of chasing my dream."

"To be a traveling journalist." he replied. "I know."

"When I discovered I was pregnant I toyed with the idea of not telling him. I knew Mom would help hide if that's what I wanted but I couldn't do that to his family, or myself."

"You couldn't be any other way."

She wasn't sure what to say to that so she slid her hand through his hair and kissed him.

THE NEXT MORNING, AS Jason lay holding Nicole, he thought again of how he worried that her run in with Clair would turn her back to her old ways, but she'd treated him no differently. During their evening stroll through the garden, they walked closely together and stopped for some sweet kisses. When they returned to his room, the lovemaking had been passionate.

But he couldn't forget the way she had been watching him the afternoon before, as if she expected him to disappear. She also seemed sad when he had found her in her room, but she hadn't wanted him to know. It could just be that she was nervous about meeting his father the next day, as she had gotten when she met his brothers.

He pushed his worries to the back of his smiled at the sight of the woman sleeping in his arms. Her hair was in disarray but she looked peaceful, almost too peaceful to wake up. He leaned down and kissed her lips lightly, running his tongue along her bottom lip until she opened her mouth for him.

He enjoyed these special moments in the morning. He pulled her closer and felt her shiver. His arm beneath her head, held her shoulders close as his other hand drifted to caress her buttock, pressing her against his morning erection.

He groaned into her mouth when someone knocked on the door. In the days they had been sharing a bed no one had ever disturbed them.

"Rise and shine," T.J.'s voice carried through the door.

Nicole shook with a giggle against his chest, as Jason told him, "We'll be down in twenty minutes."

After hearing his footsteps, rush down the hall, he joined Nicole in her amusement. He looked over at her. Her face was flushed and her lips rosy. He couldn't resist one more kiss before letting her go.

He watched her slip back into her gown and robe before slipping out of the door. As he dressed his excitement began to stir at seeing, at least, part of his family. He just hoped father and youngest son could make the drive without arguing. Having Maude as a buffer would help.

He didn't understand why the two of them seemed to fight when left alone, but act with comradery when the others were around. That was one pf the reasons the two brothers had decided to get and apartment of their own.

Dressed in jeans and a tee shirt he headed down to breakfast. Rose, Jean, and T.J. had begun eating but Nicoel hadn't come down yet. Rose mumbling, but listening he realized she was double checking a list in her mind.

"Rose," he told her, "I can assure you that it doesn't have to be perfect for them. If something is forgotten, you will be quickly forgiven."

"I can't help it." Rose spoke in a rush. "An actual Sweetwater brew master. It's the only beer my father would drink. Thomas as well, supporting local businesses." Then her voice got soft, remembering, "I would gather up Dad's cans and take them to trade for treats."

She stopped talking as Nicole stopped in the doorway. She was dressed in a pair of yellow shorts and a white shirt with yellow flowers on it.

"If I'm going to take a few more days off, I should go check in at the book store." she told them. "I shouldn't be long."

Before anyone could respond she was out of the door again. He looked around at the other's faces. Rose looked disappointed but Jean spoke up.

"The store has been her life away from the house for too long for her to go so long without checking in."

Rose nodded. "Of course, you're right. Why don't you check the guest rooms and I'll make sure the kitchen is well prepared?" Then she looked at Jason, 'I'm sure you two boys can find something to entertain yourselves."

"Of course." Jason assured her. After the two ladies had exited the room he turned to T.J., and noticing his frown ask, "Are you alright?"

The young boy nodded his head. "I thought the three of us could do something together this morning, but it's okay if it's just the two of us."

They both got up and head out back, followed by the puppy they had named Rocky, where they walked around the garden, stopping at the coy pond. The sun was bright and it looked to be a cloudless day. They finally settled on the bench.

"So, you don't mind my spending time with your mom?"

T.J. looked at him, surprise widening his eyes. "I told you I wouldn't."

Jason shrugged. "I just wondered if you had changed your mind."

T.J. shook his head and stared at the fish. "If I tell you something, will you keep it a secret?"

"You know I will. Buddy?"

"I dreamt that you were my father." The boy's voice was barely above a whisper. "That me, you and Moma were a family. When I woke up, I was disappointed. I love grandma Rose and Grandpa Thomas, but Dad never made Mom as happy as you do."

For a few moments Jason couldn't speak. Hadn't he imagined the same thing a dozen times over the weeks. Finally, he said, "You realize that family doesn't have to end in blood. You can have family of the heart, like your Uncle Charles and Aunt Summer. I would be very proud to be your father, but we can't forget how you came to be here. Maybe, one day, we can be a real family."

"And you would never leave?" the boy's eyes lit with hope.

"No, it would be the three of us, together, always." Jason replied. "Now, go get those gloves and ball so we can play catch."

T.J. gave him a hug before running back toward the house, the dog not far behind, leaving him with the feeling he couldn't express to a child. When he'd first met Nicole again, and done the math, he had briefly wondered if he could be the boy's father. But he dismissed it, knowing that Nicole would have told him. She wasn't the kind of lady to hide such a thing.

But that knowledge hadn't stopped the yearning.

NICOLE HAD KEPT HER composure for as long as she was able. She pulled into her usual parking spot and entered through the back door. She stopped and waited for Summer to see her. It only took a look and her friend was at her side.

"What's wrong?" Summer asked, taking her hand and leading her to her own office.

"I've made a terrible mistake." Nicole finally managed to say.

Stacy was behind the desk but stood immediately when they entered, leaving the open door. Summer led her to a chair by the window and told Stacy. "Get us two Irish Coffees."

With Stacy gone Nicole started without being probed, "Yesterday I ran into Clair when we were picking up some food." She recited the whole conversation. "I never even suspected..." She noticed that Summer was looking past her, out of the window. "What?"

"Last week, when Charles came home and ask how sure that you were about T.J.'s father." Summer told her. "He noticed some things while they were together."

She leaned over and nodded. "I thought that T.J. was mimicking Jason, but I realized he wasn't doing anything different. I just assumed the pill failed with David, since Jason used condoms. Besides, Jason and I only shared one night. What are the odds it being him compared to my fiancée of over a year?"

"It's understandable. A mistake anyone could have made." Summer said, soothingly, rubbing he back. "I was positive things had gone beyond just friends on the cruise, and I never thought it either."

Nicole felt herself start rocking, like when she'd been young and was upset. "I'm positive that I made a mistake now, and have to tell him the truth, but I'm afraid it'll be too much for him and he'll walk away from me. Not to mention his father and brother will be here today. I don't want to ruin their visit, but how can I keep this a secret any longer."

Stacy returned with their coffees and Summer insisted that Nicole drink. Stacy left without a question, shutting the door behind her.

Nicole hadn't realized that she'd been crying until a tear fell on her hand. "This will be so hard on Rose. She just told me she didn't know what she would do if she lost T.J. as well. For someone determined to live life without hurting anyone, I've sure made a mess of things."

"Alright," Summer set her own cup down. "Nothing is positive until there's a test done. So, I suggest that you go and welcome your guests. Then you can choice an appropriate time to explain things to Jason and suggest one."

Raising her head, she inquired, "What about Rose. If we do it here, she'll find out before we've left the hospital."

"Maybe he knows someone in the city that can do it." Summer suggested. "Now all you have to do is pick the right time to tell him."

"He'll think the same thing Clair did." Nicole moaned. "The whole town will believe I tricked David because I was going to lose him and his money."

"I've always said that you worry entirely too much on what other people will think."

"The only other thing I can think is how much happier I would have been if hadn't walk out on the cruise."

"Don't do that to yourself." Summer remarked. "We can't change the past. We can only make amends and move on."

"Since you're so full of wisdom today, any suggestions on how to tell him?"

"Sorry. You'll have to come up with that on your own."

By the time she finished repairing her make up and drove home, she felt better prepared to face his family. Jean and Rose were rushing around, triple checking everything, but she found her boys out back playing catch.

She sat on one of the benches to watch and petted the puppy. but it wasn't long before T.J. spotted her and rushed over. Jason not far behind. She ruffled T.J.'s hair, after he finished hugging her.

"I thought you would be tired of having me around so much." she teased him. "Too much of a good thing."

Jason had sat beside her and leaned to whisper, "I will never get too much of you." Causing her to giggle and T.J. to wrinkle his nose at them.

"I like having you home more." T.J. added. "It's been fun. Even if you kiss more than Aunt Summer and Uncle Charles."

Jason chuckled loudly when she blushed. She slapped his shoulder and told her son, "We'll try not to embarrass you."

"Not embarrassed. I just think it's gross."

"I'll have to remind you of that one day." Jason remarked. "You'll change your mind."

Shaking his head, the boy ran inside. "I'm going to check on my grandmas."

They shared a laugh as they watched him and Rocky disappear. When it was just the two of them, she felt Jason put a loose strand of hair behind her ear, and shivered when his fingers brushed her neck.

"Was everything alright at the store?"

"Running smoothly." she told him. "I've just never left the manager in charge for so long."

"I know you don't think they can't run the place without you, but I'm glad that you see they can."

She looked at him, puzzled. "Why?"

"I was thinking about taking you and T.J. to spend time with all of my family. Maybe middle of August."

She pushed back the thought that she may not make that trip with them and smiled. "It's sounds good."

He put his arm around her shoulders to pull her closer. "I'll let Glen know. My sisters-in-law will plan it all out and all we will have to do is show up."

"Do you realize that you plan everything in our relationship? And you're becoming a hard act to follow."

"I have a secret." he admitted. "I've been getting advice from my brothers. This wooing is new to me."

"Wooing?"

"Isn't that what they call it?"

"Yes, back in the 1800s." she giggled. "I believe it's called romancing your lady."

Now he chuckled. "I'm pretty sure that isn't right either."

"Probably not." she agreed. "Whatever it's called, I'm enjoying it."

Leaning in he replied, "Me, too." Then he kissed her. Letting herself drown in the feeling he stirred she wrapped her arms around his neck. Being in his arms drove her worries away and she was going to take advantage of it.

WHATEVER HAD BEEN BOTHERING Nicole, she had resolved it in her own mind. He wondered if she had realized she was in love with him. It had thrown him when he realized that was how he felt about her. Is that why she had run off to talk to her best friend.

He let her think she had fooled him, but she hadn't. She'd come back much more relaxed, and more affectionate, than when she had left. He didn't have time to think it through though, as his family was due to arrive right after lunch.

He could tell that Nicole had grown nervous, but she hid it well as they all welcomed his father and brother Maude hadn't been able to make it. Her own parents had arrived to spend time with her while the rest of the family were on their vacation. His father seemed struck speechless when Rose took it upon herself to show him where they could wash up from their trip.

By the time Frank and Seth were shown back to the sitting room, they found bottles and cans of Sweetwater Beer. After everyone had made their chooses the rest were taken back to the ice box.

"I can't believe an actual Sweetwater brew master." Rose was crowing. "My father and husband would be so jealous."

T.J. was beside Seth, asking questions about his high school baseball team. Jason sat observing, for the most part, happy to see is father relaxing. He'd been concerned that he would be uncomfortable around such obvious signs of money.

Nicole was quiet but watching her son interact with Seth. He took her hand, drawing her attention to him. When she gave him one of her sweet smiles, causing him to lift her hand and kiss the back of it.

He didn't miss Seth's snicker or their father's knowing stare. They had never seen him interact with a woman that he had feelings for.

After an hour of getting acquainted Jason showed Seth and their father to their rooms, just down the hall from his. Leaving Frank to settle in Jason followed Seth into his.

Seth's bag was on the bed and he went over and started unpacking, remarking, "I get the feeling that I should be looking for a one-bedroom apartment."

Jason grinned. "Things have been going well. You would know if you answered my calls."

Seth looked at him with a sheepish grin. "Sorry about that. I got busy, and knew that I would be coming to visit."

"Busy with what?"

"I've been looking onto going to college." Seth admitted.

"It's about time." Jason commented. "What are you thinking of studying?"

"You're the one that kept pressing the idea." Seth told him. "I'm taking my older brother's advice and going into Psychology."

"I am the wisest of us all." Jason boasted, and had to dodge the shaving bag thrown at his head.

"Except for when it comes to your love life." Seth pointed out. "I know you got advice from Chad."

"He was the lady's man of us all."

"If he's the lady's man, Glen is the fighter, and you're the smart one, what does that make me?"

Jason pretended to think minute, before saying, "Extremely fortunate."

Seth raised a hand holding a shoe. "Do you want this to be the next thing you have to dodge?"

Jason felt he'd hit a nerve and spoke seriously, "You're the bravest of us all. I thought you knew that."

Seth sat on the edge of the bed. "I'm not sure where you get that from."

"You have been standing on your own longer than any of us. You were only six when she left, yet you never cried for her in the night. Even when you got hurt you ran to Glen or Chris. I often wondered how you done it."

"None of you ever realized that I wasn't surprised." Seth wondered aloud. "Except Dad. All of those years he resented me, thinking I had known and didn't warn him."

"How would you have known?" Jason asked. "You were a child."

"He was right. I knew." Seth saw the surprised expression and went on. "I knew she was getting ready to run. For two years, I was in the house alone with her for most of the day. She talked about getting her GED and going to work, or attending school. But something happened at the end of the Summer and she stopped talking about it. I don't know what he said but Dad made it clear that he didn't want anything to change."

Jason was glad he had been leaning against the fire place, because he felt as if he had the wind knocked out of him. How had he not seen what was going on? Had they all been so selfish that they never considered that she had dreams of her own. How could his father have been so selfish as to know and not accommodate her?

He was beginning to see that his brothers had been right about him. Emotions were not his forte. But he was learning, through Nicole and T.J. that those thing s were important as well.

"Why didn't you say anything?"

"I felt sorry for her." Seth admitted. "She had a right to a life outside of that house. He was being selfish and I figured if she took off it was his own fault."

"What about the rest of us?"

"I figured that y'all knew. She hadn't made secret out of being frustrated at being stuck at the house while Dad had poker night and bowling night. He spent his other nights out with buddies as well. He didn't become the good father he is now until after she left."

Thinking back, he remembered the fights after bedtime. Her crying the nights he hadn't bothered to come home for dinner. He wondered if Glen or Chad knew. Why hadn't they ever talked about it?

They all seemed to go on as before, accepting that she wouldn't be back. Maybe it was time for the brothers to sit down and discuss what they each knew. Maybe he could arrange it while they were in the city next month.

Thinking again about the talk he'd had with T.J. about family he couldn't help thinking that families were becoming very complicated. Everyone walking around with secrets because they didn't want to hurt one another.

"Are you angry?" his younger brother asked.

Shaking his head, he told him, "We should have been paying attention. There's a chance our older brothers know something but never spoke up either. I was the only one walking around with a heart of ice."

Seth smirked, "I think it's beginning to thaw."

"Living with this family and seeing how they relate to each other, although they come from different walks of life. They've blended together and if you remove one piece, it's not going to be the same."

"Are you worried about finding a place for yourself?"

"No. I believe it's there if I want it."

CHAPTER ELEVEN

Over the next few days, the two families got to know one another, and Nicole was able to sooth her nerves. She still hadn't found a time to tell Jason the news but with so many people in the house it wasn't easy to be alone. And when they were together at night, she couldn't bring herself to ruin what little time she had with him.

She had watched as Seth and Jason worked with T.J. on his hitting. They were both patient and knew how to instruct him without T.J getting frustrated, which usually happened. By the time they were having their last practice T.J. could hit the ball with confidence.

Today was game day, and he'd been so excited that he'd barely eaten. Rose and Jean had ridden to the fields with her, while T.J. had piled in with Jason's family to arrive early to the field and warm up.

Now, the older ladies sat with Frank on some chairs they had brought instead of the bleachers. Summer and herself were standing closer as the captains picked teams. Since Jason was a captain, she was concerned that he hadn't chosen T.J. until he winked at her. They obviously had a plan.

"You shouldn't put it off much longer." Summer was saying, "There's always the chance that someone else will notice."

"I know." Nicole murmured. "I'm going to do it before his family leaves. That gives me two days to get the nerve up."

"He may understand, you know."

"Eventually, but at first, he's going to be angry. Like when he first arrived and learned my story."

"That's why you should do it sooner rather than later."

"If I just knew how deep his feelings ran." she replied, almost to herself.

Summer scoffed. "If you don't know that you're blind."

Before she could respond to that they were approach by her uncle and cousin. After a welcoming hug he went over to sit with Jean and the others. But Brittany stood with them, looking over the ball field.

"It least there's a breeze now and then." Brittany commented. "So, Nicole which one is your new man?"

"It looks like their team is batting first." Nicole answered with a smile. "He's the one with black hair."

Brittany looked over and seemed to pale a bit. "Who's the other one?"

"That's his brother Seth." Nicole told her. "Are you alright? You look as if you've seen a ghost."

Brittany scoffed. "Not a ghost. I met Seth a couple of weeks ago. Not under the best circumstances."

Summer looked amused. "What were the circumstances?"

"My last relationship had just ended and I was drowning my sorrows." Brittany filled them in. "He drove me home, helped me inside, and left."

Nicole and Summer's eyes grew wide. It was Nicole who asked, "He didn't try anything?"

Brittany shook her head. "Just left his phone number. We've been talking on the phone and texting since then, but we haven't seen each other since that night."

The sat on the bleachers, watching the game get started, and catching Brittany up on the local gossip. Since she started college in the city she didn't come home much.

It wasn't until it was T.J.'s turn to bat that Nicole was sent into a panic. Jason was beside him, giving him last minute advice

Her cousin leaned over and said, softly, so no one else would hear. "If I didn't know better, I would say Jason was his father."

She felt the color leave her face, and was sure she was pale as a ghost.

Brittany noticed as well. "I was kidding." Then she took a closer look at Nicole. "Is that a possibility?"

"Let me see T.J. bat and we'll go have a talk."

Brittany nodded and turned back to the field. For the next five minutes her mind was consumed with her son. He missed the first pitch, and the second was too high so he didn't swing. It was the third pitch that he hit the ball and it flew into center field. T.J. was so surprise he didn't run until Jason yelled for him to.

The kids in the outfield were so surprised to see the ball flying through the air that they were late in trying to catch it, stopping the boy at third base.

She stood up with the rest of the crowd and cheered as he made it to third base. She was so proud she could burst. After the next hitter made a base hit, T.J. crossed home plate. Jasn was waiting and lifted him onto his shoulders while his teammates cheered.

She turned to her cousin and indicated that she should follow. They walked well away from everyone else she told Brittany everything.

"I don't know how to tell him without him getting angry." she admitted.

"We both seemed to have problems with men." Brittney commented. "Maybe you should tell him you love him first."

Her heart raced at the thought, but she couldn't do it that way. "I won't tell him the first time like that."

"Maybe you could show him." Her cousin suggested. "Plan something special."

"That's a good idea." she replied. "It's embarrassing confessing all of the to you. Being five years older I was supposed to be someone you could look up to. I'm sorry."

"You have been." Brittany assured her. "And this won't change that, I'm glad to see you're not so perfect."

She nodded and inquired, "What mistakes do you make with men?"

"Keeping them at arm's length." Brittany answered. "I'm afraid that we have the same issues."

"At least you didn't marry a man you were certain you would never love."

They hugged and went back to the bleachers. Brittany's idea had some merit. She'd been thinking about doing something special for him. Something to show him how she felt since she wasn't able to tell him yet.

Then it came to her. Something he had mentioned that he'd never done, and she knew the perfect place.

T.J. WAS STILL GETTING congratulated when Seth caught his eye. His brother was looking at where Nicole was talking with another woman. He didn't recognize the woman but saw that they were in a serious discussion a few yards away from the bleachers.

"Do you know who that is talking to Nicole?" Seth asked him.

"I think it's her cousin." Jason answered, "Now you can tell me why dad has been giving me odd looks."

"Like he would tell me." Seth replied, looking back over to the ladies. "Is her name Brittany?"

Jason shrugged. "I haven't met her yet. She lives and goes to school in the city. Why?"

"No reason. She looks like someone I know." Seth remarked.

"Do you really not know why dad has been giving me looks?"

"Positive. I've noticed it, but he hasn't confided in me what's going through his mind." Seth answered. "Your lady is looking tense."

He glanced back over and saw the two women hugging. He'd noticed the same thing several times since his family had been here, but he didn't know what was causing them. He'd also noticed her watching him closely, as if she were afraid that he was going to disappear.

He briefly wondered if it had been something that Clair had said, but he didn't believe she had the power to hurt Nicole. He wished that she would trust him with more than her heart. He wanted her whole life.

He couldn't wait for them to go into the city for a few days. He wanted to get her away from this town for a while. Or Clair. She was the only thing that seemed to take Nicole's thoughts away from their relationship, the only one that didn't want Nicole to find happiness.

"What are you thinking?" Seth questioned him.

"Why is it that unhappy people want to make others unhappy? Not really other people, just one other person." He proceeded to tell Seth about Clair, and the way she seemed to enjoy tormenting Nicole.

"It sounds like she's jealous. Nicole married the man she loved, moved into the big house while Clair was denounced by her family, forced to make it on her own. By waiting for David, she probably feels like she gave up any other opportunities that she may have had then." was Seth's assessment. "Besides, misery loves company."

"Why is it that when you explain these things it makes so such sense, but when I try to think them through, I go in circles."

"Because you think logically, feelings aren't logical." Seth explained, simply.

He thought about that through the afternoon, as he helped coach the team. As a scientist he used logic to help solve problems. Emotions weren't logical, yet a great deal of people were ruled by them, made decisions around them.

That was probably why he didn't enjoy reading fiction, whose characters acted on emotion, even when facts are starring them in the face. Maybe he should try reading more so that he could start understanding people better.

Their team won the game, with T.J. hitting the ball every time he was up to bat. His friends were pleasantly surprised, as was Charles, and he'd known they were working with the boy every day.

Finding him in the crowd, Nicole stood on her toes and kissed his cheek. "I've never seen T.J. enjoy these games so much. Thank you."

He felt himself blush. "It was mostly Seth. It turns out he's a great coach."

"Should I go thank him, then." she pretended to look for his brother.

Putting his hands at her waist, he pulled her closer. "I'll pass on your appreciation."

Then he kissed her in middle of the cheering crowd. Until T.J. came running over.

"Mom, did you see my homerun." he asked. "I made a hit every time. Everybody was so surprised."

Nicole laughed and knelt down to talk to her son. As he watched the two of them, he once again thought 'what if'. He couldn't deny that he wanted this for himself- a wife and children. Now he understood his older brothers better. When you found the person that made your life worth wild you didn't want to let them go.

As they dined that night, he watched how everyone related to one another. It all seemed so harmonious, except the looks his father kept giving him, as if he wondered what was going through his son's mind.

Just after dessert Frank nudged Seth before standing up. "If you will excuse us, there are some things I need to discuss with my youngest son."

Seth tried to hide his surprise, but Jason knew him too well. He was about to follow, in case of trouble, when Nicole leaned over to him.

"I have a surprise for you. Meet me in the garden, the usual time." Then, kissing his cheek, she was gone.

So were his father and brother. Since he didn't know where they would have gone, he just hoped that there wasn't any trouble brewing between those two.

THE NIGHT WAS CLEAR, with all of the stars shining brightly, and just a quarter moon. She could smell the scent of flowers around her as she waited for Jason to join her. She stood in her robe as usual, but had a golf cart behind her, loaded with a blanket, some towels, and a basket with a bottle of chilled wine.

She was growing more nervous the longer she waited for him. She had put this together quickly, but had thought about it all afternoon. She was going to do everything she could to show him what lay in her heart, that way when she told him what she now suspected he hopefully wouldn't be as angry.

Then he came out and she smiled, welcomingly. He was dressed just as she was, but looked curiously from her to the golf cart.

Coming to stand in front of her, his arms went around her waist. "What have you got planned?"

Her hands resting on his arms she told him, "Just a private picnic for the two of us."

"Mm." he murmured, before nibbling on her lips.

She giggled and pulled out of his arms. "Keep that up and we won't make it."

He released her and they both climbed on the cart, with her driving. It took fifteen minutes for them to reach their destination. The small pond on the property. There was a field of wildflowers next to the tall pecan tree.

She carried the blanket over and laid it out while he followed with the basket. Unpacking it she handed him the bottle of wine and a corkscrew.

She took a deep breath of fresh air while he poured them some wine. "I love it out here. Sometimes when I have to get away from it all, I come here."

He handed her a glass. "Then why are you showing me?"

"Because the house is crowded and we are never assured our privacy. And I have a surprise planned." she finished her wine and stood up. She untied the robe at the waist, and let it slid down her arms, to the blanket beneath her feet. "Didn't you say you've never been skinny dipping?"

She almost laughed at the way he downed his wine and stood up before her. Any doubts that she had that her body wasn't as desirable as before giving birth were wiped away by the way he looked her body over. The heat that flared in his dark eyes was visible even in the dim light.

When he reached for her, she skipped away, laughing. "I'll meet you in the water."

As her feet entered the edge of the water, she braced for the coolness she knew was to come. But it wasn't too cold and she was soon in the water up to her waist. She turned to see that he had removed his robe and silk boxers he wore to bed.

She watched him walk toward her like a panther on the prowl, causing her body to react. Her breath hitched, nipples hardened, and warmth began to move through her. He stopped when he was standing in front of her, and this time when he reached for her, she didn't move away. Her body pressed against his as he claimed her lips for an exchange that almost set her on fire.

Pressing closer she didn't realize his intent until his arms tightened around her waist and he feel backward, submerging them both in the water. She came up from the water sputtering and trying to get her wet hair pushed back, while he came up laughing.

She laughed with him, and splashed water in his face. The splash war continued until she jumped on him, her legs around his waist, and joy in her heart. She allowed the freedom of the moment to lead her on, knowing it wouldn't last.

She held his face between her hands and kissed him with all of the love in her heart. She wanted to leave him as little doubt about how she felt as she could give him without saying the words.

Her hands moved to his wet hair, as she felt his hands begin to roam over her curves, his thumbs teasing her already aching nipples. They stayed like that for long moments just taking pleasure in being with each other.

Eventually, she released her legs and slid down his body, until she was standing on her own feet. She took him by one hand and lead him from the water, back to where their blanket waited. Letting his hand fall she picked up a towel and began to dry him off. She took her time, feeling the muscles under his skin bunch and release at her caress.

Indicating that he should sit, she proceeded to dry herself while he watched. Once done, she knelt before him, and pushed him until he was laying on his back. She couldn't tell him how she felt just now, but she showed it in the way her hands and body worshipped him as he'd done her so many times before.

The way his body responded to her, and the sound of his moans, urging her on. When his hands caught her at the waist and began to roll them, she shook or head with a smile.

Moving her hand between them, she guided his length to her entrance and lowered herself down slowly. His hands caressed her thighs and buttocks as she drove them both wild with desire.

His hands ran up her back and pressed her forward until their lips almost touched. He whispered something she couldn't make out before his hand in her hair, the other holding her around the waist, he gave her a heated kiss as he drove his hips upward, causing her to moan.

Their movements grew more frantic as they grew closer to release. Once it was over, and she was sprawled in his arms, she couldn't help but think she'd done everything she could to let him know how she felt, aside from telling him. She would give them this since of bliss for a few more moments before telling him something that could make him turn away from her.

Chapter Twelve

Nicole fell asleep in his arms under the stars. Jason didn't know when she had time to plan this, but he'd enjoyed every moment. It was as if she'd been trying to tell him something through her actions. He hoped that it was the same thing he'd been trying to show her for weeks.

He'd never felt this kind of love before, as if you couldn't survive without the other half of you. He'd observed other's, with the infliction, enough to know what it was. He hadn't tested the theory so far, but he assumed that she would even be able to draw him away from his work.

As much as he wanted to join her in sleep, he knew that she would be embarrassed to be found this way. He eased his arm from under her, pulling away. He tucked the blanket around her before pulling is boxer shorts and robe on.

He loaded everything else on to the golf cart, then went back and picked her up on the cradle of his arms.

She stirred a bit when he set her in the seat beside him. "No, there's something I need to tell you."

His arm around her shoulders, he tugged her back against his chest. "Shh. Sleep, we can talk later."

He felt the moment she relaxed back into sleep, and smiled to himself, confidant that he'd been right about her plans. If she didn't love him yet, she soon would.

He pulled the cart up to the back porch. Then he cradled her slim body against hm again, and carried her upstairs as quietly as he could. Obviously not quietly enough, he met Seth coming down the stairs.

Seth looked him over and raised a brow in silent question.

"If you help me get her to bed, I'll take a walk with you."

Seth turned around, walking ahead of him, and opened her bedroom door. Jason carried her through it and was glad to note the covering was already pulled down.

He turned his head to Seth. "I'll meet you out back."

Seth grinned and nodded, closing the door softly behind him. He laid her on the bed and unwrapped her from the blanket covered in dirt and grass. Not wanting to wake her up, he didn't dress her, but pulled the covering up over her.

He brushed a strand of damp hair from her face, and looked down at her. If he could win the heart of this beautiful lady, he would be happier than any man alive. Turning off the lamp, he shut the door and crossed the hall to his own room. He removed his rob and boxers, pulling on pair of sweat pants.

He found his younger brother on the porch, starring out into the darkness. Seth turned when he heard someone approach. Jason didn't miss the stiffening of his body as if he were preparing for an attack.

Jason held his hands up. "Sorry. I didn't mean to sneak up on you."

"You didn't. It's too quiet here." Seth complained.

"Are you talking to someone?" Jason's concerned prompted the question.

"Some days I feel like all I do is talk."

"I'm referring to talking about your own problems with someone, not you letting your buddies unload on you." Jason commented.

"I can take it." Seth replied, defensively. "Some of them came home with worse injuries than PTSD."

"I'm not saying not to be there for them." Jason spoke up, quickly. "Just that you need to take care of yourself as well."

"I know that you're right." Seth sighed, heavily. "I haven't been sleeping well at home either."

Jason nodded. "I noticed. I just hoped that it had gotten better. I've heard that a pet can help."

Seth ignored him to comment, "It seems you had a good night."

Jason couldn't stop the grin. "We were skinny dipping."

Seth turned to him, his eyes wide, "I remember you refusing to go with us."

"You were breaking into a pool we weren't supposed to have access to." Jason reminded him. "And swimming naked with my brothers wasn't worth it to me."

"And tonight?" Seth probed him.

"It was a surprise." Jason admitted. "But I didn't protest too hard."

Seth snickered. "Or not at all."

Jason chuckled. "Would you?"

"Of course not." Seth admitted. "How was it?"

Jason let himself think back over the night. "I think she was trying to let me know that she loves me."

"Hmm." was Seth's only reply.

Jason noticed the vague response. "What happened with you and Dad earlier? He looked irritated."

"You know him." Seth remarked. "When things are going well, he's sure to find a way to ruin it."

"So, something is wrong. What did he do?"

"Don't worry about it." Seth told him. "I'll take care of it. By the way, I went ahead and found a place. I'm moving next week."

"I understand." Jason told him. "You couldn't wait on me forever."

Seth nodded. "You go get some rest. I'll walk through the garden and be on up."

NICOLE LAY HALF ASLEEP, replaying the events of the night before in her mind, when she suddenly sat straight up. She hadn't told him. She had fallen asleep and he'd brought her home and put her in bed without waking her. And he hadn't joined her.

She hopped out of bed, and got dressed in a flash, but when she opened her door, she knew he had already gone downstairs. His bedroom door was open and there was no sound from within.

Going back in her room she pulled her hair back in a braid, slid into her sandles, and headed down to breakfast. Maybe she could get to him before they all got busy. The idea had barely formed when she arrived to find out he and Seth had gone to pick up some things in town.

She sat in her usual seat and helped herself to some bacon and eggs. It wasn't until she reached for a croissant roll that she noticed Frank was watching her. She couldn't keep herself from squirming under his gaze as she began to eat.

"How long will they be gone?" she tried to sound casual.

"If I know Seth, he'll keep Jason away until the guests arrive." Frank said, gruffly. "He knew I needed to talk to Jason."

She forced down the bit of eggs in her mouth. She had no doubt that Frank was suspicious. She just didn't know what to do about it. She didn't know him well enough to ask him to keep something from his son, nor did she want to. All she could hope at this point was that she could find a way to tell Jason as soon as possible.

T.J was talking excitedly to his Grandma Rose, and Nicole pretended to be listening. She could feel a sense of doom settling in the pit of her stomach. After twenty minutes she excused herself and walked out to the back porch.

The yard was filled with workers unloading tables and chairs, her mother directing them where to go. Needing to be alone she turned toward the garden.

She suddenly worried that she shouldn't have waited so long, maybe too long. Clair had only seen them together for twenty minutes at most. Now she was positive that Frank knew as well, after only a few days. How many others noticed what she had needed pointed out to her? Were there already whispers in town, that she hadn't heard.

It didn't matter if they had noticed. Clair was sure to start telling people herself. Finding joy in ruining Nicole's life is what she wanted. She didn't understand what she had ever done to the woman to earn her dislike. Maybe she should have stepped aside when she realized why David had been using her, but she'd been trying to protect herself.

She could see that now. She hadn't wanted to chance being hurt the same way her mother had. That was why she had slipped out on Jason on the cruise. She'd ran from the pain that she was about to unleash on herself, there was no one else to blame. Not even Clair.

All she could do now was keep busy and hope that she found the time to talk to him before anyone else did. Then she had to tell Rose. She didn't know which one was going to hate her worse.

She went over and helped her mother with the table covers. They worked together well, but Nicole found herself turning and looking for Jason to return, and her mother sent her inside. She considered going down to the book store but was afraid of what she would find out. She had enough to face without boring trouble.

Finally, she went upstairs and took a hot bath, that relaxed her until she went back downstairs. Guests were beginning to arrive and Jean and Rose were greeting them at the door. She began searching for her son, and found him running round out back with his cousins.

She was so surprised when Jason approached her from behind and put his arms around her waist that she jumped. He kissed her ear and whispered an apology.

"It's fine." she told him and covered his laced hands with hers. "There's something we should talk about."

He glanced around at the crowd already gathered. "Right now."

She sighed. "I guess not. It's just that I meant to talk to you last night."

"You said something on the way back to the house." he remembered. "If I had known it was important, I would have come back sooner. Seth seems to be avoiding our dad for some reason."

She turned in his arms and gazed up to his face. "I don't know how much time we have before we're disturbed, will you meet me in my room as soon as everyone's gone?"

He smiled charmingly. "If you wish."

"I do." she stretched up to kiss him sweetly.

His lips trailed to her ear. "I'm sure we could find a private spot somewhere."

She laughed and slapped his shoulder. Not long afterward, they seemed to get drug in different directions.

Through the afternoon she paid close attention to the party goers, to see if they were whispering or starring but they weren't. Apparently, Clair was keeping her suppositions to herself. Honestly, she didn't care about anyone but Jason and rose. As long as she was the one to tell Jason and Rose, to hell with everyone else.

They found a few minutes together, here and there, and sat together with T.J. to eat. She noticed that Seth was sitting beside Brittany and they seemed to be having a private conversation.

Not long after that the guests started to head out to watch the fireworks. Charles was getting ready to leave with the kids and T.J. insisted that Jason go with them to see the fireworks display.

When he came over to explain, she could tell he was reminded of their talk. "I'm sorry."

She saw Frank watching them, closely. "Just come straight up when you get back. Don't stop across the hall. I'll have everything you need."

He gave her a long kiss goodbye, and went to join the group that was leaving.

She felt guilty for enticing him that way, but it was a sure way to get his to come straight to her. She could no longer deny that his father knew, she could tell by the way he'd been watching her. She felt as if there were a bomb ticking down and she was going to run out of time.

JASON HAD HAD HIS DOUBTS about the small town's fireworks display, but it turned out to be better than he'd expected. The day had been incredible, but full, and he was ready to have some time alone with Nicole.

She'd been intent on talking with him and he was looking froward to it. She had shown him the night before how deep her feelings ran for him, and he was hoping that she would say the words.

He had some big plans for them, but hadn't wanted to rush things. This relationship may be new to them but he'd been dreaming about it for years. He had no doubt that she was his match, he'd just been trying to get her to see it.

He's already arranged to have a ring, spoken to T.J, and planned to talk to the ladies before leaving for Atlanta. Now that he knew his feelings were returned, he would plan the proposal.

T.J. had gone to find his grandmothers and he'd started up the stairs, intent to get to Nicole. He was surprised to find Seth at the top of the stairs, leaning against the wall.

His brother hadn't gone to the display, but stayed behind. He'd also been talking to Brittany most of the day, avoiding most of the crowd. Jason understood, but hadn't expected for him to be waiting for Jason to get back.

"What is it?" Jason asked, upon seeing his brother's expression.

Seth looked as if he'd rather be anywhere other than waiting on his brother, looking as if the world were about to fall apart. "I need to talk to you."

"Of course, I was just going to my room to change…" he was saying.

Seth cut him off. "My room would be better."

Jason shrugged and followed Seth, when he turned I the direction of his room. Seth opened the door and walked in first, closing the door behind Jason.

When he saw his father sitting in the chair in a corner, Jason got a sinking feeling in his gut. Frank was sitting with his arms and legs crossed, and didn't greet him when he'd entered.

He turned to find Seth leaning against the door. "What's going on?"

"You should sit down," was Seth's answer.

Jason walked over and set in the desk chair. His father was still silent, which was another bad sign. "Just tell me"

"I know that I asked this before but how sure are you that T.J. isn't your son?" Seth began. "Have you ever asked Nicole?"

"No, but why wouldn't she tell me?"

"Look around you son." His father finally spoke up. "If the truth came out, she would lose all of this. I've seen pictures. That boy looks nothing like his father, or his grandfather. The only thing he shares with his grandmother is his dark hair. I knew it the moment I laid eyes on him."

"Dad, you promised to let me handle this." Seth said, sharply. "I told you that you can't just throw things at him like you do the rest of us."

Jason felt his head start to spin as he tried to put together what his family was saying with the woman he knew. Nicole wouldn't keep something like that a secret just for the money she may lose. But he reminded himself of how much she cared about what the people town thought of her.

Shaking his head and standing up, he said "No, no, no."

That brought his father and brother's attention back to him. His felt his world spinning out of control, and he couldn't grasp what was happening.

"Do you know what T.J. stands for?" his father threw at him. "Did you even bother to ask? I thought you were the smart one."

"T.J." he whispered to himself. One thing was becoming clear, she had let him believe a lie. Taking advantage of the fact that Seth as no longer blocking the door he opened it, almost taking it off the hinges, and headed to her room.

He saw all of his dreams going up in smoke. He didn't want to believe what his father was insinuating, and he wouldn't until he heard the words from her.

He still felt as if her were watching from outside of his body. His blood ran cold in his veins. How could he have been so foolish?

When he arrived at her door he didn't bother knocking, just throw the door open, letting it crash against the dresser beside it.

"What does T.J. stand for?" he demanded.

Chapter Thirteen

Nicole was waiting in her room for Jason to return. She'd already showered and was dressed in a baby blue, satin robe that had been delivered the day before. She'd ordered it for a something different to wear for Jason. He'd once told her how beautiful she was in the color.

She was sitting at her vanity, brushing her hair, when she heard the door crash open to reveal a very angry looking Jason. Even before he spoke it was clear that she had waited too long.

He stood stiffly, eyes blazing, and nostrils flaring from heavy breathing. "What does T.J. stand for?"

She came to her feet slowly, and turned to face him before she answered, "Thomas Jason."

"Why didn't I know that?" he demanded. "Why didn't you tell me?"

"It never came up. You never ask." she stuttered, not liking his accusatory tone. "I didn't know that you didn't know."

"Are you sure it wasn't so I would guess he was truly mine?" he accused. "I never questioned it because I never would have taken you for the kind of person to keep it from me. Although I've wondered to myself, I told myself 'She would tell you if it was a possibility.' I was such a fool."

She took a step toward him. "Not as big a fool as I was."

He took a step back, shaking his head. "Only because you've been found out. You knew I would want to claim him and you didn't want to lose all of this." He gestured to the house they were in. "Why else stay in house that couldn't have good memories for you? Of course, you worried about losing your reputation in town. Why do you care so much more about what everyone else thinks more than me?"

Suddenly feeling desperate, she approached him and reached out to touch his arm, "You've got it all wrong. Just give me a chance to explain."

Shaking away her touch, he stepped back again. "It's over. We'll get a blood test done and if he's mine, I will claim him. I don't care what it does to your reputation." With that he stalked out.

Once the door closed behind him, she let herself fall onto her knees. The tears started even as she wrapped her arms around herself. Rocking back and forth, she let them fall as she tried to hold herself together even as her heart shattered.

She wasn't sure how long she sat there before the door softly opened and closed. Then her mother's arms encircled her, and helped her to her bed, where she finally let go. Held in her mother's arms she cried like she hadn't cried since she as a little girl. Hiccupping sobs that she couldn't control, with tears that wouldn't end.

After a while she grew quiet, let Jean go, and sitting up. She didn't trust herself to speak as Jean turned to the bedside table and handed her a glass. The amber hue told her that it was scotch, and she took a sip.

Jean just waited while she drank more. It seemed to steady her nerves, as it warmed her.

"It's over." she told her mother, flatly.

Jean scoffed, "Nonsense. I've never seen to people more meant to be together,"

She nodded once. "Did you know about T.J.?"

"I suspected. I was giving you the chance to realize it on your own."

"I never did." Nicole replied, dryly. "I didn't realize it until Clair accused me of getting pregnant by someone else to trap David." She gave a short laugh.

"Anyone who knows you could never believe that." Jean assured her.

"Jason does." She took a shaky breath. "He thinks I didn't tell him because I didn't want to lose the money and my lifestyle."

Her mother put an arm around Nicole's shoulders. "He spoke in anger. But why didn't you tell him right away?"

"Rose." she answered, simply, laying her head against Jean's chest. "And we were expecting his family. I thought I could wait until after the holiday. And I knew that it would be the end."

"You don't have much faith in love, do you?" Jeans remarked. "I'm sorry for that. I had hoped that you would learn from my mistakes."

"What mistake?"

Jean smoothed her daughter's hair as she answered. "Giving my heart to the wrong man. I knew that your father didn't love me. Oh, he cared for me, but he wasn't a man that wanted to settle down. When I became pregnant and your grandfather forced the issue, I thought I could love him enough to make up for what he felt he lost. It took me longer than it should have to realize he would always want his freedom."

"Mom, I know much dad hurt you and I've tried to avoid that kind of pain. But it seems I've brought it on myself."

"Love doesn't die that quickly." Jean told her. "He's angry, and when men get angry it's sometimes best to give them time to think."

"What makes you think that he loves me?"

"The way he looks at you, the way he lights up when you enter the room, but mostly by the way he treats you. He worries when he senses that something is bothering you. Someone isn't that tuned onto someone else's moods unless strong feelings are involved."

"Then why did he never say so?"

"Maybe for the same reason you haven't told him the same thing. Fear of being rejected."

Her tears began again. "I don't want to lose him."

"Then, when the time comes to talk, you can tell him everything. Things can be set right when heads are cooler." Jean told her. "Jason came by to tell Rose that he's got to go home and take care of some things. He'll be back in a few days. The two of you can have a long talk then."

"He's leaving?" she raised her head.

Jean nodded. "He's headed out in the morning with his father and brother. Don't panic. He'll be back to see things straight with his son."

"Of course." She took another deep breath. "I think it best if I'm not there. Could you say my farewells for me?"

Jean nodded and stood up. Pouring a little more in Nicole's glass, and giving it back she advised. "Try to get some sleep."

THE NEXT MORNING DAWNED cloudy, matching Jason's mood. He hadn't slept. He'd sat up to think but his anger wouldn't allow him to see clearly. Everyone had met for breakfast and say their goodbyes, except for Nicole.

He had heard Jean go to her the night before, and wasn't surprised when Jean informed them that Nicole was in bed with a migraine. He didn't think anyone else believed it any more than he did.

He missed her presence at his side. He actually had to remind himself that whatever she was going through now was her own doing. She was the one who had lied, causing everyone's pain.

Even their son's, who was probably the only one that didn't know what had happened. Although if Rose knew, she hadn't shown it in any way by word or look.

Now he knelt in front of T.J., seeing him with his eyes open. It was as if he were looking at himself at the same age. Except his eyes were the same blue as his mother's. He wanted nothing more than to throw his arms around the boy and claim him, but he knew that it had to be handled carefully. There was still too much up in the air right now.

"I have to go home for a few days and take care of some family business." it was the easiest explanation he could think to give T.J. that wasn't a complete lie. "Seth and I need to meet with our other brothers and discuss some things and we've put it off as long as we can. I programmed my number into your phone so you can call any time you want to."

T.J. nodded and wouldn't look at him but murmured. "I know there was a fight."

Jason curled his finger under the boy's chin and forced him to look at him. "I'm not going to lie to you. Your mother and I argued, but that has nothing to do with you and me. She and I had discussed my going to meet with my brothers, so I'm just giving us both a little space while I handle this. Do you understand?" He didn't mention that the two of them were supposed to go with him.

He received another nod before T.J. threw his arms around Jason's neck. He blinked back hot tears as he held his son tight. His father and Seth had already left, and he was meant to follow. After standing and saying his goodbyes to the two older ladies, his eyes wondered to the top of the stairs, half expecting to see Nicole, but she wasn't there.

He hardened his heart toward her again, and walked away, closing the door behind him.

ROSE AND JEAN STOOD in the entrance hallway after their grandson had run off to his room. Sparky, the puppy following behind. Rose felt awful for her part in this.

"I never meant for this to happen." she moaned. "I was trying to do the right thing."

Jean dropped an arm around her friend's shoulders. "No one could have predicted how he would take it. Besides, did you see him look up the stairs before he walked out. You should know better than I that love doesn't die that quickly."

She nodded her agreement but said, "That doesn't stop their hurting now."

Jean turned them both toward the living room. "Yes, she's hurt and Jason's angry, but that's a sign of the feelings they haven't revealed to each other. We'll give them a couple of days. If one of them doesn't come to their senses by then we'll put another plan in motion."

"What plan?" Rose asked her, as she took her usual chair.

Jean sat in its twin. "That's what we have two days to come up with." After they shared a conspiring grin, Jean assured her, "Nicole has never risk her heart like this before, and with their past it was bound to be trickier than we could have imagined."

"We didn't know what we were getting ourselves into." Rose agreed. "How much worse can things get?'

The housekeeper chose that moment to enter, carrying the cordless phone. "Ms. Rose, there's a call for you."

Rose put the phone to her ear/ "Hello?"

"Hello, Mrs. Rose," said a smug voice on the other end. "Have you heard the news yet? I warned her that I would be calling?"

"Yes, I heard that you ran through the money my son managed to set aside for you." Rose spoke coldly. She was frustrated and the last thing she needed was her son's mistress complicating matters further. "Why are you calling?"

Jean looked at her with wide eyes and her mouth open. Rose put a finger to her lips indicating quiet and put the phone on speaker.

"I had assumed that Nicole had told you, but no matter, I'll be the bearer of the news." Clair replied, haughtily. "Your precious grandson isn't David's son. We wondered how she had become pregnant while using protection when I hadn't when we had been trying."

"Did you honestly believe that we would have accepted you into our family because you claimed to be carrying David's child?" Rose remarked. "You are the one I would have doubted. David knew that under no circumstances would we accept you, if he led you to believe anything else, that's on him."

"Why would you believe her and not me?" Clair demanded. "I'm the one he truly loved."

"And what do you truly love?" Rose asked, in return. "Money and Power. Do you think I don't know about the other young men you tried to snag so you could live off of their family's fortunes? You may have fooled David, but you could never fool me. A mother knows."

"Fine, then. You think it's money that I love?" Clair threw at her. "Give me two million dollars, or I'll let everyone know about your so-called perfect daughter-in-law. You will no longer be able to proudly claim that kid as your blood."

Clair didn't know it but she had just struck on the one thing she was afraid of, losing the right to be in T.J.'s new life. But she wasn't going to bow down to this woman's blackmail.

"Listen very closely to what I'm about to say because I will only warn you once. If you so much as cause, Nicole or my grandson any pain, for any reason, and I will use every dime of this money that you so crave to ruin you. You want be able to sell yourself on the streets when I'm done with you. Do you understand?"

After a long silence Clair spoke one word, in a defeated voice, before hanging up. "Yes."

Rose ended the call and set the phone on the table between them. She buried her face in shaking hands.

She felt Jean's hand on her head. "You're not going to lose him. Thank you for standing up for her."

Lifting her face, she whispered, "T.J. isn't the only one I'm afraid of losing. Nicole is like a daughter to me as well."

"I know that she sees you as a second mother. If she hadn't loved you and your Thomas so much, she would have left David years ago."

"But when she finds out what I've done, she'll be angry." Rose countered.

Jean snickered before saying, "Do you think she and I never fought? That I never done something that caused her pain. It's partly my fault as well. Family isn't perfect. We hurt each other sometimes, but we also forgive each other, knowing the other person only had the best of intentions."

"I hope that you're right."

CHAPTER FOURTEEN

It had been two days since she'd watch Jason drive away from her bedroom window, and she still hadn't left her room. People came in and out, delivering trays of food or trying to entice her to go outside, or at least down stairs.

She didn't want to eat, everything tasted like sawdust in her mouth. She couldn't motivate herself to even read a book. She felt as if a part of her was missing and she couldn't survive without it. All she did was lay in bed and think about what could have been.

What if she hadn't slipped out of the room on the ship? What if she had considered, just once, that she could be carrying Jason's baby? What if she had gone straight to him when she'd first realized the truth? Every version ended happier than this one had.

There was a soft knock on the door and she bid them to enter. Opening her eyes, she saw T.J. standing beside her bed.

"Hi, Little man, what are you up to today?" she asked him.

"I wanted to talk to you about Jason." He climbed up to sit on the edge of her bed.

She ran her fingers through his wave black hair. "What about Jason?"

"He gave me his number so that I can call him," he told her. "But I don't want to talk to him. I'm mad at him."

She studied his expression. "Why are you mad at him? He explained that he had some family things to take care of."

"I know that you two fought and his going away has made you sad." He looked solemnly into her eyes. "I'm not going to talk to you him as long as he's making you sad."

She hugged him, tightly, for his loyalty, but she couldn't let him continue to blame his true father. She released him and crossed her legs Indian style.

"Come on. We need to talk." She waited for him to turn and face her, imitating her sitting position. "T.J., I'm going to talk to you like a grown up, because I believe that you can handle it. But I'm going to have to ask you to keep it a secret from grandma Rose for now, okay."

His full attention was on her now, sensing how serious this discussion was. His eyes were on her and his hands in his lap.

She took a deep breath and wondered where to begin. "Do you remember hearing about me attending your aunt and uncle's wedding?"

"On the cruise." he said.

"That's right." Nicole continued, "I met Jason on that trip." She almost laughed when his eyes widened. "That's right. Can you imagine our surprise? We spent a lot of time together on that trip. I think a part of me feel in love with him then, but I had already promised to marry..." she stammered not knowing how to refer to her late husband in this situation. "David. We parted and I never expected to see him again, we exchanged no contact information.

"I returned home and soon learned that I was carrying you. I was so happy, and never doubted the right thing was to marry David, assuming that he was your father."

She waited and watched as he accessed the situation. Seeing the truth light in his eyes as she grew nervous about his reaction.

"Is Jason my dad?" he asked, hesitantly.

She nodded. "I never questioned who your father was until someone pointed it out and I didn't tell Jason right away. That's why we fought. He was angry, rightfully so, and needed some time to think. The reason he was angry was because he feels that I was lying to him, that I'd kept his son from him on purpose. I want you to understand that."

"Grandma Jean says that sometimes when men get angry, they need time cool down." T.J. replied. Then his eyes dropped. "I dreamed that he was my real Dad. Now my dream came true but I still don't have a dad around."

She felt tears sting her eyes and blinked them back. "He'll be back. There's no way he'll stay away from you now."

He looked at her again as if something else just dawned on him. "That means that grandma Rose, isn't? Are we going to move away from her?"

She rubbed his arms with her hands before he got to overwhelmed. "I don't know anything yet, but I don't believe that she would ask us to leave. She will still love us."

His breathing steadied and he nodded, "Family of the heart. That's what Jas....Dad called it."

"That's why I know he'll be back." she assured him. "So, maybe you can call him. I won't feel hurt, I promise."

"I'll think about it." he promised. "But are the two of you still going to be a couple?"

"I don't know." she said, trying to keep her voice from wavering. "That's for the two of us to discuss. You aren't to worry about it."

"Okay. I'm going to do some studying."

She was able to hold the tears back until the door closed behind him. For him to want someone as a father other than David spoke volumes to her. Had she buried herself in work so much that she hadn't realized how David's behavior affected her son. She had believed that the love he was given from the rest of them would make up for it. It was one thing for her not to realize what David had done to her self-esteem, it was another not to notice how it affected her son.

How many more mistakes had she made that she hadn't realized the consequences of? She fell back and rolled over to bury her face in her pillow.

THAT'S HOW SUMMER FOUND her the next day. Curled on her side, sobbing her heart out into her pillow

She knew it was Summer when she replied, dryly, "Well, I never thought I would see the day."

"What day is that?" Nicole couldn't help but ask, her voice shaking.

"The day that I would have to pull you out of bed." Summer informed her. "You done it for me often enough as teenagers."

Nicole felt her sit on the side of the bed she was facing.

"I was right. Love isn't worth it." she mumbled int her pillow. "That's why I ran from it."

"Girl, you weren't running from love, you were running from the pain it can cause." Summer retorted. "Now, sit up so we can talk. Your mother has assured me that she'll help drag you up if it's needed."

Taking her time, Nicole sat up and pushed her hair out of her eyes. "Fine, but I'm not going anywhere."

"You're not going to find a solution sulking in this room." Summer reminded her, soothingly. "You have a family counting on you. It causes them pain to see you this way."

Looking to her bitten down nails, she told her. "I can't seem to make myself care. Maybe I was better off before I realized how lonely I was."

"Why don't you call him?" her friend suggested. "He's probably sitting in his father's house just as miserable as you are."

"That's just it. I caused all of this misery. I deserve what I'm going through, he doesn't deserve to go though it as well." Nicole felt the tears slid down her cheeks. "I've hurt him twice now. I have no reason to believe that he would give me a third chance."

Leaning forward, Summer wrapped her n a hug. "Why are you convinced that you're doomed when it comes to the heart."

She snorted. "Look at all of the mistakes that I've made."

Summer pulled back to look in at her. "That's only because you were too busy studying to make them when the rest of us did."

She couldn't help the smile that appeared on her face. "One of us had to be sensible."

"Thank you for holding off on making mistakes so you could take care of me." Summer stuck her tongue out at her. "You could at least take a shower."

"Just don't leave." Nicole insisted. "I think I want to talk."

"I'll be right here."

Nicole stepped into her bathroom and quickly showered, washing her hair as well. The hot water helped to relax her and she was feeling slightly better when she stepped out, wrapped in a fresh robe.

Summer was sitting on the bed but she'd left to go get them some coffee. She handed Nicole her cup as she settled back on the bed. Slowly, she told Summer everything that had happened since they had last spoken at the barbeque.

"I can't believe that he thinks I'm the type of person to deny a child his father so I could keep a fortune." she finished.

Summer was shaking her head. "That's probably something his father put in his head. But why didn't you tell him who you were really worried about? Not David, but Rose."

"I tried but he wouldn't listen." her voice quivered. "He said that he couldn't stand to look at me."

"He spoke in anger." Summer spoke from experience. "Men talk about women bringing up the past, but they're just as bad."

"I'll wait for him to calm down and return." Nicole told her. "Then we can talk about what to do about our son."

"But what about the two of you? You're not giving up."

"I'll leave that to him." Nicole repeated the words given to T.J. "I'll do what it takes to make things right, but I'm not getting my hopes up."

"Or we could go into the city and tie him down until he listens." Summer replied, and laughed.

Nicole knew that her find was only half kidding. If she'd decided to go in the middle of the night Summer would be by her side. But Summer knew that when Nicole had made up her mind about something, she didn't change it.

After finishing her coffee Summer left to return to the shop. She hadn't asked what people in town were saying. It didn't matter. No one mattered but Jason. Funny how what had become so important to her meant very little at the moment.

Nicole sat and thought about the things Summer and her mother had said, trying to give her hope. Her heart wanted to grab on to that hope, but her head knew it wasn't that easy. Love may not die that quickly, but a person can only take so much before they gave up.

She decided then that she would apologize, tell him she loved him, but she wouldn't do anything until he came back. The decision was up to him. She would hold a little hope in her heart, just not enough to cause too much disappointment.

SUMMER DIDN'T LEAVE right away. Instead, she headed down to Rose's library where the other two ladies were waiting.

Rose sitting in the right, wing chair, Jean in the left. She sat in a chair nearby, facing the two.

"She's gotten a shower and drank some coffee." Summer informed them.

"Is she going to call Jason?" Jean asked.

Summer shook her blond head "I think the three of us need to share information now. The first thing is that there is a good chance that T.J isn't David's son..." she stopped when Jean and Rose shared a look. "Both of you know?"

"Yes." Jean as the one to answer. "We figured it out after she told me who Jason was, but she didn't seem to know. Never considered the possibility."

"And never would have if Clair hadn't accused her of getting pregnant by someone else to trap David because she sensed she was losing him." Summer told them everything. "She was worried how Rose would take the news. Jason saw it as her putting David's memory ahead of him in her mind. Do either of you know how his father was so positive.

Rose looked down and told her hands, "We had been trying to give her time to see on her own, what we saw, but I made a mistake. At the barbeque I called My grandson over to me, 'Thomas Jason' Even as I realized what I had done I thought it may be a good thing that Frank seemed to notice, but I never expected it to turn out like this."

"Of course, you didn't." Jean reached over and patted her hand. "And you more than made up for that mistake when you handled Clair"

"What do you mean?' Summer inquired.

"She called Rose." Jean explained. "Trying to make Nicole look bad so she would like the one that really loved David."

"I let her know what would happen if I found out she was causing Nicole more trouble."

"Thay explains her deciding to go back to the city." Then Summer asked, "Rose, are you all right with this? Nicole was so worried how you would take it."

"It's not easy, but it doesn't change how I feel about either of them." Rose told her. "I don't want to lose my grandson, but I'm more worried about our Nicole and Jason. The first thing we need to do is get them together. We can discuss the rest then."

"How do we do that?" Summer inquired. "I could send Charles to drag him back."

The way they both smiled told her they knew she was only half kidding. Then she had a sudden idea.

"I'll get him back here." she told them as she stood. "But, Rose, you need to tell them what you know right away. They're going to have enough to work out."

Rose just nodded. Summer knew how difficult this was for her. She would make sure that Jason did as well.

"What are you going to do?" Jean asked, looking concerned.

"If she won't go after him, then I will on her behalf." Summer told them. "She's done it for me."

It didn't surprise her to find T.J at the front door. "Are you going to help?"

"Yes, I am. Maybe you can help too." She knelt down and the two of them whispered back and forth. Then she ruffled his hair, "Don't worry. This will work."

He gave her a hug and she was on her way.

CHAPTER FIFTEEN

They had been at home for three days when Seth's phone rang with an unknown number. He answered in case one of his Army buddies was calling with a new phone. He couldn't have been more shocked when it turned out to be a woman,

"I don't know if you remember me but I'm Nicole's friend, Summer. I need to meet with your brother." the feminine voice practically demanded.

Not liking her tone, he responded, "You'll have to be more specific since I have three."

The woman sighed. "I'm sorry. I had a hard time getting your number from Brittany. She only agreed because I'm trying to help him and Nicole."

He stood from his chair as if he'd been called to attention. As he walked toward his bedroom, he said, "It couldn't hurt for you to try. I haven't been able to talk sense into him yet."

"Hmm. Your being helpful all of a sudden." she remarked. "Could it be because Brittany blames you for letting your father tell him nonsense."

"That could be part of it." he admitted. "But I do like seeing my brothers happy."

"Can you set up a way for us to meet, without him knowing I'll be there."

"Just let me know when. As long as you get Brittany to come as well."

"I'm sure I can arrange that." Summer agreed. "I've arranged to leave work early today. I can be there around five thirty."

"Alright. We can meet then at McHenry's Bar. Brittany knows where it is."

"One more thing." Summer's voice hardened. "I'll get you a meeting with her but that means if you ever hurt her, "I will make sure you regret it."

"Understood. See you soon." He hung up. His feelings uplifted as he changed into fresh clothes. It wouldn't be hard to get his brother there, but he believed that Summer had her work cut out for her.

JASON WAS SITTING IN his room trying to read, but he couldn't concentrate. He'd lost his appetite, and when he managed to fall asleep. he woke missing her in his arms. In the three days he'd been home he hadn't heard from anyone in New Hope. Not even T.J. had called, as he'd hoped he would.

Parting from Nicole this time hurt worse than the first. He knew it was because he'd gotten a glimpse of what life with her would be like. His chest felt hollow as he wondered again if he should have given her a chance to explain. He worst thought was that she didn't have a better explanation, and that's why she hadn't bothered to call.

There was a sharp knock on the door, before it was opened to reveal Seth. He shut the door behind him and leaned against it.

"Dad still raging?' Jason inquired.

"Yeah, but I'm use to that." Seth told him. "However, Brittany called and abused my ear for half an hour before hanging up on me. Now she's declining my calls and texts."

"Sorry." Jason apologized, then wondered why he had.

His younger brother continued to stare at him. "What are you reading?"

"Harry Potter." Jason answered, only slightly embarrassed. "We were reading them but it's not the same."

"Why not?" Seth remarked. "The words are the same."

Jason thought about it before answering, "I think it's her voice. She was reading them aloud to T.J and I started listening as well."

"She still reads to a ten-year-old?" Seth remarked "That's odd, especially considering his IQ."

"It's how they spent time together." Jason found himself explaining. "Even when she'd busy at the shop she comes home at lunch on Friday and they spend the afternoon studying the arts. Mostly literature."

"It doesn't sound as if you still hate her." Seth observed. "Maybe it's time to go back and get answers, maybe a paternity test."

Jason closed the book and laid it on the table beside him. "Are you trying to get rid of me?"

"Of course not, but we've talked to Glen and Chad and now know everything it's possible to know about why Mom left,"

"I don't need a test." Jason closed his eyes and pictured his son. "He's my son. I have no doubts. I don't believe, as dad insinuated, that she kept it from me for the money. She is overly concerned with how people see her, but not enough to keep this from me."

"There's only one way to find out, my brother."

"I'm not ready to talk to her yet."

"So, you do still hate her?"

Jason groaned and laid his head back against the headrest. "It would be easier if I could hate her. Even when I was so angry at her that it hurt, I worried about how she was after I left."

Seth chuckled. "Nothing about love is easy."

Jason didn't bother to deny it. "How would you know?"

"I observe people and I remember what our older brothers went through."

"I still feel like I will always be second in her mind. She seems to consider everyone's feelings but mine." Jason told him. "I thought that I was making some headway with her, but this situation makes me think I haven't. I thought she wanted to confess that she was in love with me. I thought that's what she had been trying to show me the night before, but it turns out she was trying to make up for lying to me."

"Maybe you have to make the first move." Seth suggested. When he received no reply, he straightened into a standing position. "I'm headed down to the bar. You should come with me."

Shrugging, Jason put his book aside and changed shirts. It couldn't hurt to get out and be around happy people.

Since it was the beginning of happy hour, the bar was starting to fill up. All kinds coming in after work to have a drink before heading off to have dinner; from mechanics to personal assistants.

Jason and Seth were sitting at a table in the back of the bar, which seemed odd to Jason since he knew that Seth was hoping a certain lady showed up.

He told himself he'd just come to keep his brother company, but it was really to get away from his father's constant lecture about how he should be claiming his son. He didn't need the lecture. Nothing would keep him from T.J. now. He just needed enough time so that he was sure he could keep his heart of stone around Nicole.

He took a drink of beer and wondered what she was doing. Her life had probably just gone back to normal. He knew now that he would never be first in her heart. There would always be a ghost between them.

He'd had such high hopes for them. It had seemed as if they were growing closer. She'd began sharing more of herself with him, more of what she felt, or so he had thought.

He came back to the present when Seth suddenly spoke, "There they are."

Jason looked at him in confusion. "Who are?"

Seth jerked his head in the direction of two women walking toward them. He had no problem recognizing Summer, and soon saw her friend was none other than Brittany.

He turned back to his brother. "What's going on?"

"Well," Seth stood and helped Summer into a seat. "Summer wanted to meet with you, and you know I've been trying to reach Brittany. We just did each other a favor."

Then he led Brittany to another table close by, giving each privacy of a sorts. Jason looked at his love's best friend.

"Can I get you a drink?" he waved over the waitress.

As soon as she placed her order and the waitress was gone Summer said, "Why surprised to see me? Surely, you understood the last time we spoke alone."

Jason hadn't forgotten their meeting in the hallway the night she'd brought Nicole home. "I thought there had been a warning hidden in there."

"You're not going to ask how she's doing?"

"Since you're here, I assume not good." Jason replied dryly. "What about how I'm doing?"

Summer raised a blond brow. "Well, you're dressed and not hiding in your room."

Jason felt as if his heart had stopped. "What are you saying?"

The waitress returned with Summer's drink and disappeared again.

Pausing to drink, she finally answered. "She hasn't left her room... no, she hadn't left her bed until yesterday. I finally talked her into a shower, but she went straight back to bed."

He couldn't imagine his Nicoel just lying-in bed, and letting the world go on around her. She was always on the move, even when she was supposed to be taking a break from work.

Summer continued in his silence. "She was planning to tell you about T.J., which she had only figured out a few days before. Her hesitation had nothing to do with David, but everything to do with Rose. Did you realize that Rose has no close family left?"

"What do you mean?"

"She has some cousins scattered about but no siblings. David was her only child and he's been gone for ten years, along with the love of her life. That's why she clings to T.J. so much. Nicole was worried about what it would do to her spirit and health when she learned he wasn't her blood."

"I had no idea." Jason muttered. It was becoming clear to him now, the dilemma that Nicole had faced.

"Not to mention that Clair was the one to point it out to her." Summer kept talking, fiddling with her phone under the table. "I know that the two of you have other issues, things that need to be said, but I'm positive if the two of you are honest with each other you can work it out. Especially since Clair will no longer be a problem."

"How do you know that?"

"She made the mistake of calling Rose. She didn't know that it was Thomas that kept her from confronting the woman before the accident. After there was no reason, until now."

It was true that there were things that he'd kept her from knowing, and clearly there were things she hadn't revealed yet. His heart now fluttered like a butterfly. Was it possible that he'd been right all along, that she was falling in love with him?

His phone vibrated in his pocket and he pulled it out. Seeing the name, he didn't bother asking Summer to give him a minute before he answered

CHAPTER SIXTEEN

"Hey, Little Man. How's it going?"

"Alright, I guess." T.J. said. "I've been reading the book we were on."

Jason couldn't keep himself from smiling. "Me, too. How far have you gotten?"

They discussed the book and what they had read on their own. He saw Summer get up and take her drink to join Seth and Brittany.

"I miss story time." T.J. suddenly admitted. "I know I'm too old to be read to but I like Momma's voice."

"Have you asked her to continue?" Jason spoke, ternately.

"She's been sad. Spending all of her time alone." He heard the sorrow in his son's voice. "She'll feel better when you get back, Daddy."

Jason was sure that his imagination was playing tricks on him. "What did you call me?"

"Daddy. Momma told me that's who you are."

"She told you?' Jason repeated after him.

"Yes, sir. It was alright, wasn't it?"

Covering his eyes and squeezing back happy tears he assured him. "It's perfect."

"So, are you coming back?"

"I always intended to come back."

"And you'll make Momma happy again?"

Jason wanted to tell give his son everything to make him happy but Jason wouldn't lie to him. "I hope so, but she and I have a lot to discuss. Not all of it is about you, son."

"When will you be back?" T.J. probed. "There's something I've been wanting to give you."

Suddenly Jason couldn't wait to be on the road to New Hope. "I'm on my way, but don't tell your mom."

"I promise. I love you, Daddy."

And, just that quick, he was blinking tears back again. "I love you, too, son."

He pressed the end call and stood. When he walked over to their table each waited for him to speak.

"Could one of you lovely ladies give my baby brother a ride home?" He smiled charmingly. "There's somewhere I've got to be."

Seth sighed heavily. "I take it I should start looking for a one bedroom."

Jason slapped him on the shoulder. "I hope so." Then he turned to Summer, "Thanks for coming. You're a good friend and I owe you one."

She smiled, sweetly. "I may take you up on that."

He drove toward his childhood home, meaning just to grab something from his room, but his father took notice.

"What's the hurry?"

"I've got to get back to New Hope." He tossed out as he passed through the living room.

"Finally going to claim your son." Frank replied. "I told you that you should have never left without him. She'll find a way to deny us access."

Jason stopped at the hall entryway. "She would never do that. There's more to this story than you know."

"I know that she knew enough to name him after you. Why else would she do that?" Frank shouted.

"I don't know." Jason admitted. "But I'm not going to make the same mistake you made."

Frank glared at him. "What mistake is that?"

"You never listened to Mom or considered what she needed to be happy. If you had given her a little freedom from this house, she may still be here." Jason remarked, hotly. "You can blame her, but you will cease blaming Seth. He's the one that lost the most. If you ask me, you should take a long hard look in the mirror."

He retrieved his item from the night stand and was on his way out when he spotted his father in his chair, looking defeated. He went over and knelt in front of him.

"Dad, we love you and are glad that we had you but you can't continue to take your anger out on everyone else. I know you have a reason to your anger but find a way to work through it. If you, don't you will always be angry."

His father's eyes shone with tears but he managed a smile, "Go claim your family."

Jason knew that this time his dad meant more than T.J. "Even Rose."

"Especially Rose. No one should be alone." Frank told him. Then shrugged at his look of surprise. "I go to know her well."

Jason shook his father's hand and headed to find his future.

ROSE RECEIVED A CALL from Summer and waited in the Living room. T.J. had gotten Nicole to go down to the library, the excuse being he wanted to talk to her about what he'd been reading. To Rose's surprise she'd been dressed in a simple sundress, it was an improvement over the robe, that was for sure.

She was so nervous that she was picking at her nails, an old habit from her teen years. She wanted her daughter-in-law to find happiness, she just hoped that happiness didn't cause her to lose her grandson.

Jean was at work, so she was alone for this. She soothed herself with some sherry as time seemed to pass much too swiftly, and he was at the door.

She welcomed him with a smile. "It's good to see you. Did you get everything settled with your brothers?"

"Yes, we did." with his hands on her shoulders he leaned down to kiss her cheek. "It's good to be back."

She smiled wider and touched her cheek that he kissed, and teased, "With a welcome like that I may have to send you away more often."

His head tilted he teased back, "Is that how you won my father over. You flirted with him."

"At least with him it's not a wasted effort. He's not taken."

"Yes, do you know where she is?"

"She's in the library with T.J." she said and started ahead of them. "I'll provide a distraction for him."

The door to the room was open, and T.J had been watching for them. Spotting Jason, he got up from the floor and ran directly to him. Jason knelt down and caught him in a tight hug.

After the two of them had a whispered conversation, Jason stood and starred over to where Nicole now stood in front of her chair. She saw the longing mixed with doubt in both their eyes. and saw that it was time for her confession.

She took T.J.'s hand in hers and looked down at him, tenderly. Then she spoke to them, "Before the two of us disappear, there's something I need to tell the both of you. I know the truth about T.J. That he's not my David's son. I saw it almost right away. I sent Jean to talk to you that night, to confirm that it was possible.

"I know I should have spoken up right away, but I didn't want to lose him any sooner than I had to. I'm sorry."

Jason looked at her in clear confusion. "Why would you lose him? You love him and want only what's best for him. Why wouldn't I want someone like that in his life."

"But surely you want him to recognize your family as such. Uncles, Aunts, Cousins, and an interesting grandfather."

He touched her shoulder. "But he still needs a second grandmother."

"That's right." T.J. said from her side. "You're my grandmother in my heart. That's how Dad explained it to me when I wished..."

Jason understood why he'd stopped talking and covered it up. "That's right. When your family of the heart, it can sometimes mean more than blood. You earned the right to be his grandmother, not to mention how you handled Clair."

Nicole spoke for the first time. "What does he mean?"

"She called me the day Jason left. I don't have to tell you what she said, I believe it's what she threatened you with." When Nicole gasped, she rushed own. "Short story is that she's not going to bother any of us anymore. I hear she's going to move back to the city, taking her sister with her."

"Rose, I'm so sorry. You shouldn't have had to deal with that." Nicole replied.

Rose grinned, "Oh, it was my pleasure. Now I believe my grandson and I will see what we can find for a snack."

AS T.J. AND ROSE LEFT the room Nicole sunk back to her seat on the small sofa in a sort of numb shock.

First, Jason had shown up, standing in the doorway. She had wanted nothing more than to run into his arms as T.J. had. Instead, she stood and watched him interact with their son. He looked so handsome in a pair of grey dockers and green shirt.

Then, Rose had admitted to knowing the truth about T.J., had known before she herself had. Lastly, Jason had welcomed Rose as a grandmother for T.J., just as she'd hoped he would. Was this a dream?

Looking up at Jason's tense face told her otherwise. He crossed the room and sat next to her on the sofa. Now it was time for her explanation.

"I really didn't know, Jason." she started.

"When did you find out?"

"Clair pointed it out to me when we picked up that order. I didn't know she was even there but she'd been watching the two of you. I felt as if we were being watched in town, now I believe it was her." She answered. "She accused me of the same things you did, that I had known and used the pregnancy to tie David to me. If she had only known."

"Known what?"

She looked into the brown eyes of the man she loved. "That I was about to call off the engagement myself when I found out I was pregnant. I never considered the possibility that it was yours. We'd only been together one night and used condoms as well as my pill. One form of birth control failing I could believe, but the odds..."

He nodded. "The odds were narrow."

Her tension eased a little. "When I realized that I had been mistaken, I knew that I had to tell you. Then I thought about Rose. T.J. was the only close relation she had left and I was sure that it would crush her."

"You're right. It would have. Anyone could see she how much she loves for him." Jason agreed. "What did you think I would do?"

"I wasn't sure. I was going to tell you that night by the pond, but you let me fall asleep. I knew your father was seeing the truth and hoped to tell you before he did. That's why I wanted you to come straight to me."

"But Seth and Dad intercepted me." Jason finished. "I still have one question."

"What's that?"

"If you didn't consider me the father, why is his middle name Jason?"

"I named him after the two most honorable men I'd ever met." was her simple answer.

Before she realized his intent, he leaned forward and pulled her into his arms. Then his lips were covering hers and she melted against him. He didn't hate her and she just may be on the way to a happiness she'd never expected.

When they parted, he asked, "How about a walk through the garden? There's something that I want to show you."

She just nodded as he took her hand and pulled her to her feet. There was still something she needed to tell his as well.

JASON COULDN'T GET over how good it felt just to be in her presence again. The pressure in his chest had eased upon seeing her, as if a great weight had lifted. He didn't miss the shadows under her eyes, but she was still beautiful to him.

Their hand's still clasp together, he led her into the garden, on the path between the Roses and Jasmin. The night was clear, the stars easy to see.

"If things had worked out differently, and you had broken your engagement, would you have looked for me?" he asked her.

"I don't know." she seemed to think it over. "Eventually, I would have. The reason I left the way I did was because the things you made me feel scared me."

"You didn't want to go through what your mother did." Jason repeated what Susan had said.

"I always said that I was afraid of being like my father, who hurt everyone that loved him." she explained. "Now I know I was running from anyone that could hurt me that way. The funny thing is, I've felt that pain now, but I brought it on myself."

They came up on one of the benches, in a circular clearing in the garden. He stopped and point up at the stars. "The brightest star, right there, is the North Star. The two constellations circling it represent Princess Andromeda and Perseus. The princess was very beautiful, so much so that the Queen bragged that she was more beautiful than the daughters of Poscidon.

"Of course, this angered King Poseidon, and in punishment he sent the sea monster, Cetus to destroy them. Princess Andromeda's father believed that by sacrificing his daughter, he could send Cetus away satisfied and saving his people.

"As she was being offered to the sea monster Perseus, who was flying home after a grand adventure spotted the princess and fell in love. Approaching the king and queen he struck a deal with them- he would destroy Cetus and in return he would get to marry Andromeda.

"Upon completing his promise, he learned that the princess was promised to another. The two men fought and after winning Perseus and Andromeda were married and live happily ever after. They were all placed in the sky by the Gods. The Queen was placed upside down in punishment for her vanity." he finished. "It's my favorite love story."

Her eyes lit up worth her smile. "You told me that story the first night we met."

"I know." He led her to the bench and they sat. "I fell in love with you at first sight that night as well and nothing could have kept me from spending as much time with you as possible, even an engagement ring. I never meant to keep that bargain."

As she sat in silence, taking in what he was confessing, he reached around and extracted the small photo album from his waist band. He handed it to her to pursue under the pale light post from nearby.

"I had these printed as soon as I got home and carried them on every trip. Seth gave me the book for them a couple of years ago. This is why Glen referred to you as the one that got away. After completing my doctorate, I went to work with F.E.M.A., traveling to disaster areas in hope of finding you. Not that I wished a disaster on you, but so that I would have another chance to tell you what I should have said then." He waited for her to look up at him before saying, "I love you. I knew that I would never find anyone else that understand me the way you seemed to."

She smiled. "That leads to my next confession."

He touched her cheek tenderly, "What is that?"

She touched his cheek. "I worried that you would be torn away because you felt the itch to travel again."

"Why is that?" he asked.

"Because with you my life took on more meaning, the world is brighter," she smiled, teasingly before adding. "Because I love you more than I ever thought possible."

Taking her in his arms, he kissed her softly, meaningfully, before releasing her. Sliding off of the bench, he got soon one knee, and took her hands in his, "My dear, Nicole, will you do me the honor of becoming my wife? I want to go to bed with you ever night, knowing that you will be there in the morning. I want to live happily ever after with you and give T.J. plenty of siblings."

She eyed him speculatively. "What if I were to tell you we may be on the way to one of those things already."

He felt his eyes widen so much that they stung. "Are you saying what I think you are?"

She nodded and answered. "We may want a short engagement."

He stood, gathering her in his arms, and swung her around. When they stopped turning, he didn't let her down, instead cradled her in his arms. When he began to carry her inside, ignoring her protests, he kissed her.

He didn't let her down until they were in the entrance to the living room, where everyone seemed to be waiting, expectantly. Once on her feet she smiled at their family.

"Do you want to tell them?" she asked.

He grinned and turned to the others and announced, "Nicole has agreed to be my wife. And we'll be getting married right away."

Rose sputtered. "Why the rush? We could plan...."

Jean was the one to cut her off, "Because they're giving us another grandbaby."

Nicole gasped at his side. "How did you know? I just found out."

"I'm a nurse, besides being your mother." Jean replied, then grinned. "I didn't even need to look in the bag Summer sent over."

"Next weekend." Rose exclaimed, suddenly. "We'll have the wedding here. Jason can call is family."

Then Summer looked at him, with hopeful eyes. "We could do it in the garden."

The garden, where they had declared their feelings for each other. "I can't think of a better place."

The way her eyes lit up told him that she understood. "Is that a yes?"

He nodded before looking at Rose. "I hope you know what you're asking for."

Rose came over and kissed his cheek. "The more family you bring, the happier I will be. Welcome to our family."

CHAPTER SEVENTEEN

The next day was the beginning of what looked to be a hectic one. Jason was greeted by many congratulations when his family arrived. T.J. was amazed and happy to be greeted by so many cousins. Nicole had been nervous to meet the other two ladies of the family but was hiding it well.

Seth arrived an hour behind the others and pulled him aside to give him a velvet box. "I had to wait for the inscription, but it's ready."

"Thanks. I wouldn't trust anyone else with this." Jason told him. "That's why I was hoping you would be my best man."

Seth's eyes lit up, and he smiled boyishly. "I would be honored."

"We put you in the same room as before." Jason shook his hand and put the box in his shirt pocket. "If you will excuse me, I have a meeting with two old birds."

Seth chuckled as Jasin walked away. It was good to hear his younger brother laugh. He hadn't done it nearly enough since being home.

He found Jean and Rose in the upstairs study. They each sat on opposite a small table with a lamp between them. He'd never been in this room before but he understood it was where the older women used for private meetings.

"Good afternoon, ladies." He greeted them and sat in a highbacked chair facing them. "I realize that, in the excitement, I failed to come to the two of you and ask permission."

Jean was the one to speak up. "It's not necessary."

"Jean, you raised her mostly on your own and Rose loves her as her own child. I owe both of you the respect to do this." Jason paused and tried to come up with what to say. "When the two of you decided to play matchmaker, I don't know what the tow of you expected to come of it. Did you want her to understand it was alright to move on, or did you expect her to fall in love?"

"Yes, we hoped she would learn to move on." Rose answered. "As for the two of you falling in love, all we could do was hope."

"The two of you are responsible for me finding the love of my life again." he started. "I fell in love on that ship, then she disappeared. All of the traveling I've done was in hopes of finding her. I will love her the rest of my life if you will give us your blessing."

"You have it, my dear boy." Jean said. "And I want the two of you to move to our old house. You won't have to pay anything but it has to stay in Nicole's name."

"I understand but you have to let me pay you something for it." Jason insisted. "I was able to save most of my salary and sold a couple inventions to the government before retiring my position."

"Use it for repairs or additions." Jean told him.

"How about if I pay for you to take a vacation?" He nodded his head in Rose's direction. "Maybe enough to take a friend along as well."

She seemed to like the idea given the grin she gave him. "Sold."

When Rose started to protest Jean and Jason, both stopped her.

"You're going." Jean said

At the same time Jason said, "You deserve a vacation."

They all laughed together. He pulled the box from his pocket, opened it, and showed it to them.

"Seth just delivered this." he told them. "I had special ordered it before I went home."

They both exclaimed how gorgeous it was before he put it up, "Any ideas on how I can get her alone?"

As it turned out they had plenty.

ONCE JASON'S FAMILY arrived, they didn't have much time alone, except when they were in bed. These days she was asleep before he climbed in, but woke in his arms every morning. At least the morning sickness hadn't kicked in yet.

Everyone was gathering for supper in the dining room but she'd gotten a note from Jason to meet him in the garden. Clearly, he'd been craving a few moments alone as well. She'd went and changed into a sundress of spring green, and sprayed on some vanilla perfume,

He was waiting on the back patio, looking handsome as ever in his dockers and button-down blue shirt. She walked quicker and he welcomed her into his arms, giving her a kiss that showed her how much he'd been missing her as well.

She moaned her regret when he released her. He chuckled, took her by the hand, and led her down the steps to the waiting golf cart.

"Where are we going?" she asked him as she took her seat.

"I planned a special supper for us." he told her, getting in behind the wheel. Then he leaned over for a soft kiss. "Some time alone."

"Mmmmm. Sounds good."

When he put his arm around her, she laid her head on his shoulder. It only took a few minutes for her to realize where they were going.

Tilting her head up to look at him she inquired, "Are we having another picnic?"

"Is it still a picnic if you have a table and chairs," was his response.

That's when she spotted it and sat up straight. A small wood table with a chair on each side under the shade tree. As they parked a few yards away, she saw a vase of flowers and a couple of unlit candles.

They met in front of the cart and he put his arm back around her shoulder and led her forward. Also, on the table were to covered plates, glasses and a bottle of sparkling cider.

"What's this all about?" She sat as he held her chair.

After taking his seat, he told her. "I realize that we have some things to discuss before Saturday. I'm sure that you agree."

She nodded her agreement. "I was beginning to wonder if your family was going to give us a moment alone."

"No one expected you to go to bed so early." he commented. "Is everything alright?"

"The tiredness hits me early." she explained. "Soon the morning sickness will hit."

"I'm glad to hear it's not here yet." He uncovered the plates and set the lids aside. "I had this made special for us tonight."

"Chicken Parmesan." She murmured. At the one dinner they shared on the cruise he'd ordered the dish for them. She inhaled and smiled. "It smells good."

"I'm glad." Then he opened the cider and poured them each some. "I met with Jean and Rose to ask for their blessing."

Her fork stopped halfway to her mouth. "I was raised a southern gentleman and it was necessary. They're the heads of your family."

"I assumed they approved."

"Oh, yes." he replied. "Your mother is giving us her house. I offered to pay her but she won't except anything other than my bribe to send her and Rose on a vacation."

"Really?"

"As I explained to them, I saved most of my earnings, as well as selling my rights to some inventions. I'll need your help picking out the perfect spot for them to vacation."

"So, we'll be moving?"

"Not right away, but they thought we would want our own place." he told her. "It was their idea."

Noting the concerned tone, she was quick to assure him. "It's fine. I was just thinking that was one of the things we needed to discuss, but it's already decided. What about your job in the city?"

"I'll commute. It's just forty-five minutes."

She flashed back to the blue lights flashing as they pulled up. To the officers at the door telling them there had been an accident. To the shock at learning that father and son were killed on impact.

"You've grown pale." Jason remarked, moving around to kneel in front of her to take her in his arms. "And you're shaking."

Taking a couple of deep breaths, she tried to think of a way to explain without him thinking the wrong thing.

"Another early sign of my pregnancy is getting emotional." she began, "But my mind flashed back to when Thomas and David didn't make it home. I'm sorry, but it seems to have created a fear I hadn't realized until now." She looked into his eyes and caressed his cheek. "It would be ten times worse if I lost you because you have my heart."

He kissed her tenderly, holding her face in his hands, and assured her, "As you hold mine, I will be extra careful on my way back to you every night."

She nodded before putting her arms around his neck and hugging him close. Once he was back in his seat, she decided to tell him what she had found out.

"I've been looking into changing the father's name on our son's birth certificate." she explained. "We'll need to get a blood test and present it before a judge, who will approve the change."

He raised a brow and paused before asking, "You would do that?"

"Of course. He's your son and you have the right to claim him in every way." She didn't understand why he was surprised. "Why would you doubt it?"

"Because word is bound to get out if we do that, and you would worry about what everyone was saying." he replied. "I don't want you to worry about anything but having a heathy baby."

She reached to cover his hand on the table. "I can't apologize for how I use to think, but I can tell you now that I don't care what anyone else thinks. When I thought I had lost you, I realized the only opinions that really mattered are my families and true friends."

His face brightened at that and they finished their meal. He poured them a little more cider as the sun went down. She was gazing over the small pond, watching the sky turn to orange and yellow when she noticed that he's moved to kneel before her again. This time on one knee with a ring box in his hand.

"What is this?"

He gave her one of his sincere smiles. "I love you more than I ever thought I could love anyone. When you walked away, I vowed that somehow, I would find you again. Just when I had given up, fate intervened and we found each other again. Will you do me the honor of my wife."

"Yes." she whispered as he slipped the ring on her finger. The ring was a simple gold band with a cluster of emeralds surrounding a diamond. "It's beautiful. When did you have time to get this?"

He stood, pulled her from her chair before sitting in it and seating her in his lap. "This is a copy of the ring my grandfather gave to my grandmother. Seth brought it when he came."

Looking at the ring again, she realized something. "If this is a replica, when did you start having it made?"

She could see him blush in the dim light. "I talked to Seth about it after they met you at the bar. When I found you, I wasn't letting you get away again. This is where I belong, with you in my arms."

He touched her lips to his ear and whispered, "There's no other place I'd rather be."

Chapter Eighteen

True to her word, Rose had shown nothing but enjoyment at having all of the children around. She arranged activities for every day. Their favorite seemed to be the giant inflatable water slide she'd rented for the week.

Rose was so happy that when Nicole mentioned the plans to get Jason put on their son's birth certificate didn't upset her.

Only saying, "Of course, it's the right thing to do." Then she was off with the children again.

Her mother had taken the week off and glued herself to the side of Chad's pregnant wife. They had joined in some of the planning activities, but the woman needed a lot of rest being as far along as she was.

Now, Nicole stood in her room, in a cream, sleeveless dress, gazing at herself in a mirror. She hadn't seen Jason since dinner the night before, everyone keeping with the tradition of the groom not seeing the bride before the wedding.

His brothers had taken Jason out, she didn't know where, and she heard them coming back in the wee hours of the morning. She wondered what kind of shape he must be in.

When her mother and Rose joined, with T.J. in a grey linen suit. They had debated on how to include him in the wedding. They decided that, although his grandmothers were giving them both away, in a sense, that he would walk her down the aisle as well as present the rings when prompted.

Rose came over and gave her a long hug. Drawing back Nicole noticed tears in her eyes.

"Is something the matter?"

Rose shook her head. "Everything is perfect. Those precious children just ask if they could all be my grandchildren.

I knew there was a reason you were meant to become my family, and now I know why."

She felt tears sting her own eyes. Rose must have seen them as well, because she quickly handed her a handkerchief.

"None of that now." Rose told her, "This is a happy day and they are still pictures to be taken."

Then Jean approached to hug her and straightened her veil. "We both know that I never thought David was worthy of you. Jason s worthy of you and this is the happiness I always hoped you would find. Trust in your love for each other."

Nicole laughed a little as she wiped away a fresh set of tears just as Summer and Brittany arrived. They wore dresses in the color of gold, but each a different style.

Although the wedding was an intimate affair of just Twenty people, most of whom were about to be family by marriage, she insisted on having both friends at her side.

The whole town was talking, some speculating since their trip to the hospital for a blood test, but it didn't matter what anyone was saying. The family didn't discuss it with anyone else, leaving the town of New Hope to draw its own conclusions.

She was a woman in love with a man that made her heart leap when he looked at her. She wanted nothing more than to spend her life showing him all of the joy that he tended to overlook in life, him and their son.

JASON STOOD IN THE center of the garden, Seth at his side, looking at the clouds forming in the sky. Rain wasn't in the forecast but an evening shower wouldn't be out of the ordinary in this area.

Seth put a hand on his shoulder. "Don't worry. Everything will go as planned."

"Thanks for allowing one of your duties as best man to given to T.J."

"He needs to feel as much a part of this as possible."

Jason smiled at his younger brother and looked around. The family was sitting off to the side, waiting on everything to begin.

The justice of the peace approached them and shook hands and taking his position under the archway covered in honeysuckle.

Giving him a thumbs up from behind the archway, Glen started the music the couple had selected. Brittany walked out first, in her off the shoulder dress she'd chosen. Behind her was Summer in a simple gold sundress, tied around the neck.

As they took their places Jason's eyes were still on the isle, where his family would approach. Then they stepped from behind a rose bush. T.J. was dressed in a suit, the exact copy of his own, and walked straight and proud at his mother's side.

He took it all in. Her cream-colored dress suited her pale skin better than white would have. It was sleeveless and showed the single string of pearls around her neck. Although the dress came to her ankles, there wasn't the extra weight of a train behind her. She had her strawberry blond hair up, with a few tendrils loose, and decorated with some white flowers.

When she was standing in front of him, it took all of his will power not to kiss her. He settled for taking her hands in his and bringing them to his lips as T.J. slid into his spot between the couple and his uncle.

"Who gives this lady to this man?" the justice asked.

"We do." Two female voices said in unison from the family area.

As the ceremony went on, Jason starred at the woman that owned his heart. She was beautiful and smart, obviously she was too good for him. The fact that she loved him as well made him the luckiest woman on the planet.

Time came for them to exchange rings and Jason turned to their son. T.J. proudly placed the rings in the justice's hand. He gave Jason the ring to place on Nicole's finger first.

"I was told earlier today that a Matthews man only falls in love once. It must be true because you captured my heart the first night we met. In the time we were apart I traveled the country for my career but I searched for your face in every crowd. Fate gave us a second chance and I swore to myself that I wouldn't lose you again." He slid the ring on her finger. "I'll love you all of our lives."

He saw a tear slip down her cheek as she took the ring meant for him. He was amazed to see that it was his hand that was shaking as she held the ring at the tip. "When we first met, you made me feel emotions that scared me. I realize now that I had spent years guarding my heart, so that I would never be hurt. I gave my heart to you as well, only I didn't see it until I saw you again. It was as if it started beating again. I came back to life because without you I wasn't really living."

Sliding the gold band in place she smiled at him so tenderly that he forgot about waiting for permission. He took her face in his hands and kissed her with so much laugh that it took a moment for them both to hear the laughter.

T.J. was heard grumbling, "Not this again." Causing a fresh round of laughter.

He finally felt as if he'd found where he belonged, and his life was full.

Epilogue

One Year Later

The past year had brought a few changes. Although they didn't live in the big house any more, they still showed up to eat a couple of nights a week. T.J. went their every day after school since Nicole insisted on staying until closing at the book store.

Jason was enjoying his position as Professor of Environmental Physics, and Nicole had ceased worrying so much about the commute. The biggest and best change had been the birth of their daughter, Jeannette Rose. With soft red hair and blue eyes, she was the picture of her mother.

The people of New Hope were still speculating about T.J.'s paternity but they ignored it and lived for the present and worked toward building their future.

They had put off their honeymoon until now. Nicole hadn't wanted to leave the baby, but he booked the cruise ahead of time. They were on the same ship they met on all of those years ago and it brought back lots of memories.

He had left her I the dining room to use the bathroom and came back to find the table empty. It didn't take long for him to find her out on the deck with the breeze in her hair and looking out at the stars

He approached her from behind and slid his arms around her waist and she leaned back against him.

He stroked her hair. "I had wondered where you had gotten off to."

She turned in his arms so she could look up at him. "I needed to some fresh air. I see it didn't take you long to find me."

He chuckled and tilted her face up to his. "I just let my heart lead me."

"You have to tell me how that works," she teased.

"Easy. You take part of my heart when you leave my side," He spoke as if teaching his students. "The portion I'm still in possession of simply guides me to the missing piece."

She giggled. "I'm sure that our son could argue that logic."

"Only because he hasn't learned that love has no logic." he explained. "He'll understand when he's older."

"I feel sorry for the poor girl." she murmured. "She'll never know what hit her."

He tipped her face up and kissed her lips. "Is that how you felt?"

"I still do." She looked around them. "I know that I was a bit nervous to leave but it has been nice to be with you like this without the constant interruptions."

"It certainly is. What do you say we go to our room and take advantage of all of this privacy?"

"I thought you would never ask."

Don't miss out!

Visit the website below and you can sign up to receive emails whenever Wendy Varnadore publishes a new book. There's no charge and no obligation.

https://books2read.com/r/B-A-LUTN-XUSNB

BOOKS 2 READ

Connecting independent readers to independent writers.